AF485761

A story of friendship, love, and making peace with the world you'll leave behind.

DO NOT GO GENTLE

a novel

ALLEN SHAY

Do Not Go Gentle
Copyright © 2026 by Allen Shay

All rights reserved.

No part of this publication in print or in electronic format may be reproduced, stored in a retrieval system, or transmitted in any form or by any means, electronic, mechanical, photocopying, recording, or otherwise without the prior written permission of the publisher.

NO AI/NO BOT. The author does not consent to any artificial intelligence (AI), generative AI, large language model, machine learning, chatbot, or other automated analysis, generative process, or replication program to reproduce, mimic, remix, summarize, or otherwise replicate any part of this creative work, via any means: print, graphic, sculpture, multimedia, audio, or other medium. We support the right of humans to control their artistic ability.

This is a work of fiction. Names, characters, organizations, places, events and incidents are either the products of the author's imagination or are used fictitiously. Any resemblance to actual persons, living or dead, or actual events is purely coincidental.

Editing, design, and distribution by Bublish

ISBN: 979-8-89989-132-8 (paperback)
ISBN: 979-8-89989-131-1 (eBook)

Do not go gentle into that good night,
Old age should burn and rave at close of day;
Rage, rage against the dying of the light.

. . .

Good men, the last wave by, crying how bright
Their frail deeds might have danced in a green bay,
Rage, rage against the dying of the light.

. . .

(Dylan Thomas, "Do Not Go Gentle into That Good Night")

Albuquerque, New Mexico

August was coming to an end, and the summer was turning out to be unbearably hot. The smoke from the latest West Coast wildfires had finally moved farther east, leaving behind a city struggling with its environment and the impact this was having on its residents.

John Eastman was sitting patiently in a waiting room at the University of New Mexico Hospital following his examination. In his hands, he held a book he had been reading to take his mind off the reason he was there. The book was about the planning and politics that had eventually resulted in the D-Day invasion of France. John had been a history major, and he had always been fascinated by how this particular global conflict had dramatically altered the world and the role America would play in it following the war.

John's father had been a twenty-one year-old bomber pilot during that war, something John had always been proud of, although his father, like many of those who fought in World War II, had preferred not to talk about that chapter in their lives.

He closed the book when he heard his name called and walked back to the oncologist's office. He was not optimistic.

John sat down in front of the desk while Dr. Martin spun around his monitor to show John the image on the screen.

"Mr. Eastman, I am afraid the tumor has begun to spread, as we suspected. You can see its fingers beginning to appear here on the left side of your brain. This would explain the increased severity and frequency of your headaches."

John looked at the image, then back at the doctor. There was an uncomfortably long silence.

"I realize this might be a bit of a shock to you, and I am sure you have many questions. But before we get started, I would like to let you know what your treatment options are. Normally, this type of glioblastoma is best addressed with surgical removal of as much of the tumor as possible, followed by chemotherapy and radiation therapy." Dr. Martin then gestured to the monitor with his pen. "In your case, however, as we discussed when your cancer was first diagnosed, the position of the tumor would make surgery very difficult and could result in partial paralysis or serious cognitive impairment. My recommendation to you is that we begin an immediate round of both chemotherapy and radiation to see if we can slow this tumor's growth."

John looked carefully at the image again, then sighed.

John Eastman was a lawyer. Unlike many of his peers, he was neither flashy nor verbose. He was known for his calm and deliberate manor, which he used very effectively both inside and outside of the courtroom.

He replied to the doctor in the same calm yet deliberate voice he often used when addressing a jury. "Would I be correct in assuming, from what you just told me and from what you haven't told me yet, that this brain tumor is eventually going to kill me? If that is indeed the case, I would greatly appreciate it if you could give me an idea of approximately how much time I have left before I die?"

Dr. Martin hesitated for a moment, clearly caught off-balance by John's demeanor and the directness of his question.

"Mr. Eastman, I am afraid that glioblastoma in general has a very poor prognosis. The average survival rate following a diagnosis like yours is about sixteen weeks. However, that can potentially be improved with an aggressive treatment program."

John took a few moments to absorb that information, then said, "Doctor Martin, as you know, my wife passed away from breast cancer after months of chemo and radiation treatments. Would I be correct in assuming that I should be prepared to experience similar side effects if I choose the treatment path you are recommending, and would I also be correct in assuming I would end up spending a similar amount of time in hospice prior to my death?"

Once again, Dr. Martin hesitated before replying. "That is difficult to determine. Not everyone responds the same way to these treatments."

John nodded. "I only have one last question at this time. If the average survival rate is sixteen weeks and if I take every drug and treatment currently available, how much more time can I potentially buy myself? And please, do not equivocate," he added, holding up a hand. "I simply want to know the possible maximum time I might remain on this earth, based on statistics and not based on optimism."

Dr. Martin sighed heavily, then looked John directly in the eyes. "Mr. Eastman, with aggressive treatment and considering your otherwise excellent physical condition, I believe you could potentially double that sixteen week average survival rate."

Upon hearing this, John lost interest in continuing the conversation. He stood up from his chair and held out his hand.

"Thank you for your help. I will discuss this with my family before deciding how I want to proceed."

Dr. Martin seemed relieved John had taken the news so calmly. Shaking John's hand, he said, "I'm truly sorry about the diagnosis, Mr. Eastman; however, my team and I are committed to your treatment and will provide you with the best care modern medicine has to offer. In the meantime, take this." He handed John a new prescription for a much stronger painkiller that would help him to deal with his recurring headaches and warned him to follow the dosage and frequency limits carefully

John thanked him again, left his office, and stopped at the pharmacy downstairs to fill the prescription before he walked to his car. He knew he probably should not be driving anymore, due to the growing severity of his headaches and the momentary disorientation they caused, but he had needed to do this hospital visit alone.

His first thought was to return to his law firm's office, even though he had nothing on his calendar for that afternoon. A year ago, just after these headaches had begun, he had started the process of turning over his duties as senior partner to his daughter Kate. Since this doctor's appointment had been a covert operation, listed on his calendar as a "lunch meeting with a friend," and since he was not interested in sharing what he had just learned with anyone yet, he went ahead and got into his car and drove home.

John's house was a large two-story Western-style home; much too large, he knew, for a seventy-two-year-old man living alone. When he arrived, the house was as it always was these days—dark and quiet. Despite all the cajoling from his two daughters, he simply had not had the heart to sell it and move in to something more manageable. This house had been where he and Wendy had begun their lives together, where they had raised their two daughters. Being in it brought him closer to the memories of those times and of her. Recently, however, those fond memories had been overshadowed by the painful ones of Wendy's battle with breast cancer, a battle she eventually lost.

He walked to the kitchen and pulled out a bottle of water from the fridge so he could take his medication. The severe headaches were coming two to three times a day now and lasting longer, usually at least twenty to thirty minutes at a time. He looked at the new pill bottle in his hand and realized for the first time that these painkillers were nothing more than a powerful Band-Aid. Based on the images Dr. Martin had shown him, it was clear these headaches would not only continue but actually get much worse until the end finally came.

John knew what the time between now and his death would be like, if he followed the treatment plan. He and his daughters had suffered through this with Wendy, and he could not ignore the irony that it would be his fate as well if he took his doctor's advice.

But John had no intention of turning himself over to the doctors and living with the consequences of the recommended treatment. He remembered too well the trauma both he and his daughters had lived through with his wife's cancer. He remembered not just her physical suffering but the anguish she felt knowing her last few weeks of life were bringing so much pain and heartbreak to those she loved so dearly.

He sat at the kitchen table and sighed. He knew what he had to do next. What he needed to figure out now was the how, where, and when.

John had always been a thoughtful planner, meticulously mapping out the cases he prosecuted or defended and executing them flawlessly with the same quiet but confident demeaner that had garnered him the respect of both his clients and the other attorneys he so often bested.

After graduating from Davidson, a small liberal arts college on the outskirts of Charlotte, North Carolina, with a degree in history, he decided to become a lawyer, like so many of his other classmates. One of his favorite books and movies had been *To Kill a Mockingbird*. If there was one character he would never forget, it was Gregory Peck's Academy Award-winning portrayal of Atticus Finch, which he saw for the first time in a film studies class at Davidson. It moved him and made it clear in both his mind and heart what kind of a lawyer he wanted to be.

After taking a job with an existing firm when he left law school, he realized after a few years that for him to have the kind of career and practice that he wanted to have, he would need to start his own firm. He was joined in that effort by two like-minded coworkers, and he never looked back as his new firm grew steadily and much faster than he had anticipated.

"Well, counselor," he said out loud to himself, "you know what must be done. Let's get to work."

As his current headache subsided, the clarity of his plan began to take shape. The objective was clear, as was his timeline. John was not a selfish man; however, he wanted to give himself one last chance to revisit both a person and a place he loved.

He made himself a sandwich, took a beer from the fridge, and walked toward the back of the house to his home office. He sat down at his desk, logged on to his computer, and got to work.

He left his daughter Kate a message, saying that he had been invited to a three-day golf weekend with some friends in Santa Fe and that he would not be coming back into the office until Monday. He also told her that his headaches were getting better and that he would catch up with her at the office Monday morning. He knew Kate was currently buried in two big cases she had taken the lead on, so not needing to check in on him this weekend would probably be a relief.

Buying himself these three days without contact from Kate or from his office would enable him to deal with his terminal prognosis in the way he felt was best for both him and his family. The trip he was planning over the next three days was going to be a difficult one, but it was one he wanted to take. However, its success depended in large part on the phone call he was about to make.

Chevy Chase, Maryland

Peter Grove had always been a stickler for detail when packing for a trip. In truth, he had always been a stickler for detail about almost everything. He had promised to catch the early flight to Albuquerque in the morning, but first he had to compile his list of all the things he needed to do and to pack before his departure.

He was planning on taking his three-day backpack as luggage. He had used this bag on many hikes over the years and had a special fondness for it. After a hectic and stressful life, he had found spending time in the wilderness to be a tonic for him. After decades of frequent global travel, he cherished the short drive into the Appalachian Mountains and the companionship of their hundreds of beautiful trails. Unfortunately, these hikes did not address his biggest problem—in fact, they probably contributed to it.

Peter was a very lonely man. This was surprising, considering his outgoing personality and the decades during which he had been surrounded by family, friends, and coworkers.

After finally laying out all physical items on the bed, he went downstairs to his office and began to work on the list of digital items that needed to be taken care of.

Peter had just turned seventy-two and had spent more than forty years working in the tech industry, and his home office reflected it. The shelves on both walls bordering his desk had as many antique computing devices as they did books and framed photographs. There was the 1964 electromechanical adding machine he had traded in to sell one of his first tech company's three-hundred-dollar electronic calculators. On a shelf across the room stood a leather binder stamped with the Department of Energy program logo, presented to him and his team by the head of Los Alamos National Laboratory after they installed what was then the world's most powerful supercomputer. His wide desk and wheeled chair gave him access to his laptop, his high-resolution scanner, and his video recording gear. Labeled thumb drives, notepads, and chargers were scattered around the desk. This room was the only cluttered space he allowed himself. Every other shelf, cabinet, or storage area in the house looked like an upscale department store display.

Peter's home was pretty typical for a retired senior technology industry executive who had worked with the government for nearly four decades. His house was on the outskirts of Washington, DC, and he lived alone. It was a gated townhouse community with beautiful, well-kept landscaping. The homes belonged primarily to retired couples who now spent most of their time at their second homes, on a golf course somewhere in Florida, or visiting their children and grandchildren wherever they lived.

While this neighborhood was lovely and quiet, it was not really a community. Most people living there had never even met their neighbors. They came and went almost exclusively through the opening and closing of their garage doors. The country club this development was built around was over a mile away and was surrounded by hundreds of much larger single-family homes on one-acre lots.

Peter had ended up here after his divorce twenty years ago. His wife, Karen, had left him the year after their daughter Morgan graduated from college. That was also the same year his son Scott had completed his MBA.

There had really been no good reason for Karen to stay in their marriage. She had lost Peter after 9/11 to his obsession with his job. Karen was a talented woman, with much to offer, who found herself living with a man who, for the last decade, had made little effort to be part of her life. A few years ago, she had remarried a doctor she'd met at the hospital where she worked.

There had been no animosity in their separation and eventual divorce, and Karen had more than compensated for Peter's lack of attention to his children during their early adult lives. He understood she had every right to find a man who would be part of her life, not just drop in unannounced from time to time.

For fifteen years following the attack on 9/11, Peter had led his company's government division through a maze of classified programs designed to apply and adapt their state-of-the-art software technology to stop the next big terrorist threat. He had traveled the world, helping to set up what were usually covert local data collection and analytic systems. These were being used by America's rapidly expanding Department of Homeland Security, now laser focused on foreign terrorist threats. He'd believed what he was doing would help save lives.

When he finally took early retirement and left the company following its acquisition, he could not say for sure whether they had actually saved any lives. He was quite certain, however, that the life he once had lived had been lost.

Finding himself no longer in a leadership role anywhere but in his own life, Peter faltered. He had lost his ability to find and make new friends, and his old friends had mostly forgotten him. Now, he lived each day with the consequences of putting job and mission ahead of everything else in his life. This awareness hung around his neck like an albatross. He had become just another old man living alone.

This was why the call he had just received was so important to him.

The irony was that Peter had been a good father, a good husband, and a good friend while the kids were growing up. Despite the work hours and business trips during the early years of his tech career, he'd rarely missed one of his kids' field hockey, lacrosse, or football games. The annual family ski trips and weeks at the beach, which began when his daughter was just four years old, had been something he'd always made a priority. Looking back now, he was happy he had at least given his children a childhood and adolescence filled with his love and these memorable family moments.

Their last family beach trip had been in August 2001.

The following month, planes crashed into the Twin Towers and the Pentagon. This horrific event not only changed the trajectory of his life but eventually turned him into more of a memory than a man to both his friends and to his family.

Recently, he had tried to reconnect with this two children. His son, Scott, had embraced this effort, but unfortunately, he now had his own heavy workload to deal with. His daughter Morgan was married with two young children and taught at a University out west. She also had tried to reconnect with him but she had very little time available at this point of her and her families very busy life.

Reconnecting with family and friends had become even more difficult when he discovered he was now a recipient of the Grove family curse.

It had started in earnest just over a year ago. Peter had noticed he was beginning to find it difficult to remember the names of places and people he should've known quite well. He realized it wasn't only his short-term memory faltering; memories from his past—ones he believed were permanent—were beginning to fade as well.

Peter's father, aunt, and grandmother had all suffered from dementia. All three had been in good physical health but had spent the last several years of their lives in a senior care facility, unable to recognize the members of their own family. This cognitive decline had played out differently for each of them. His grandmother and his aunt both lived the last years of their lives quietly, never leaving the grounds of their twenty-four-hour-care center. Peter's father had suffered a version of the disease that resulted in a shorter lifespan but included moments of both confusion and intense anger. The two years before he died, Peter's dad had become someone whom no one in the family recognized.

While Peter was helping to care for his father after a surgical procedure, his father suddenly erupted in anger and called him an ugly, stupid bastard. Peter knew his dad no longer knew who he was, but even so, the look of rage on his face had been difficult to forget.

Peter had gone to a doctor over a year ago, when his memory problems started to bother him, taking his first cognitive test and MRI. He was told his memory issues were common for someone his age, particularly for someone who had led a busy and challenging life.

He'd gotten a very different message when he returned for the same test and another MRI three months ago. He had struggled through the memory test, as he'd known he would, but it was the results from his latest MRI that had been the most disturbing.

Indications of small vessel disease, which could lead to vascular dementia, had appeared in the latest scan. This was the form of dementia his father had been diagnosed with. There was no cure, and he was told progression was inevitable.

The doctor's only recommendation for deferring what was now unstoppable was to eat a healthy diet and exercise—two things Peter already did and had done his entire life.

Peter now knew how his life would end. He was destined to live through the same cognitive decline his relatives had. And since he could afford it, he would most likely spend the last years of his life in a lovely senior care facility, completely unaware of where or who he was.

He had decided not to share this recent diagnosis with his children because he did not want them to worry about him. His son Scott spent enough time interacting with him, though, and Peter had found it difficult to hide his memory problems from his son. Instead, he just downplayed the severity. When he stopped midsentence because he could not remember a place or a name, he told Scott it was just part of getting older.

Sitting at his desk now, Peter suddenly felt his adrenaline flow in a way it had not for years. He had a new mission, but unlike past missions in his life, this one had nothing to do with trying to help end the threat of nuclear war or domestic terrorism. This mission was about helping a man, who had been his best friend for most of his life, end that life on his own terms.

There was absolutely no way he wouldn't honor that request.

Albuquerque, New Mexico

During the flight to Albuquerque, Peter had time to focus on his memories of John and the times they had spent together.

Peter and John had met fifty years ago at preseason football training camp at Davidson College. Often referred to as one of the "Ivy League of the South," colleges, Davidson had many students that came from Southern prep schools, and its student athletes were just that first—students. Other than a few basketball players, almost no one came to Davidson expecting to become a professional athlete. Most came to become doctors, lawyers, ministers, and perhaps someday captains of industry.

They met the first day of a three-week training camp. Peter was coming from a large high school in a commuter town in north central New Jersey. John arrived from a smaller town forty-five miles outside of Columbus, Ohio. Peter had been a defensive end in high school. John had played several positions but had been recruited to play linebacker.

He and John had bonded quickly during their first few days at camp. They both came from middle-class families and had gone to public schools, unlike so many of their formerly prep school classmates. Over the next four years, that bond would grow to the point that most of their teammates just assumed they would be best friends for life.

Preseason football camp at Davidson was a grueling experience. High heat and humidity and three two-hour practices a day left most players several pounds lighter a week in, despite the efforts of the more than competent dining hall staff to keep them at their playing weight.

As it turned out, Peter and John's freshman class at Davidson would be a class remembered as the last of an era in more ways than one. Davidson was at the time the smallest college in America playing Division 1 college football. The school's total enrollment was only one thousand men. Davidson's football program officially dropped out of Division 1, ending their football scholarship program at the end of their sophomore year. Fortunately for John, Peter, and the other recruited players from their class, they were able to keep their football scholarships as long as they continued to play.

Davidson had also been an all-male college since it was founded in 1837. Their class also turned out to be the last all-male one. The following year, Davidson went coed in an attempt to both diversify the student population and to eventually expand the school's enrollment by 50 percent, to over 1,500 students.

Their sophomore year would also be the last year the football team would be led by a man who had been a legend at Davidson, first as a player and then as the head coach. Their final two years, the school de-emphasized the importance of their football program in more ways that just financially. In their junior year, the football team while still playing mostly Division I schools was left to struggle under the leadership of second-tier coaches. By their senior year, Peter and John and a few remaining classmates had to face the challenge of being the only team in their conference with just one remaining class of scholarship athletes.

Peter thought that it was interesting how the team's struggles had affected him and John—or more accurately, how it had not affected them.

Winning only five games in their last three years had been hard on the team and its players. New coaches who blamed and belittled players and were actively trying to run off those they had not personally recruited had made the situation even worse. Realizing college football was no longer a priority made it easy for players not on scholarship to simply quit the team and focus on their studies.

John and Peter were unique because they had both decided to simply ignore the negativity that surrounded them and focused on playing a game they both loved. The game of football challenged them physically and mentally like nothing else in their lives, and every snap of the ball was another chance to show they were up to that challenge. The overall deterioration of the quality of their program didn't really bother them that much nor did the losses. All that mattered was the opportunity to line up against other college players and to win as many of those one-on-one battles as they could.

As their teammates had predicted they would, Peter and John would remain best friends—for the next twenty-five years.

———

After Davidson, Peter had returned to New Jersey and married Karen, his high school sweetheart who was heading off to med school in Virginia the following year. John was his best man.

Peter returned that favor three years later when John graduated from law school and married Wendy, who was in a graduate program in public health at the same university.

Wendy had been student council president and homecoming queen at John's high school. She had also been dating a good friend of his since ninth grade. In his second year of law school, John had looked up one day from his table at the school library and was surprised to see Wendy walking toward him with a wave and a big smile on her face. She'd sat down at his table and began a conversation that led to their first date, and the rest was, as he described it to Peter simply fate.

These were the days before mobile phones, so keeping in touch was not that easy for Peter and John. It involved long-distance phone calls you had to pay for and actual letters and cards in the mail. Despite their busy lives, they still managed to remain close. When their children were young, they decided to plan an annual weeklong ski trip to Colorado as a way to not only maintain the friendship but to extend it to their families. These trips continued for well over a decade, until the year after Wendy was diagnosed with breast cancer. The end of the annual ski trip and Wendy's battle with cancer made maintaining their friendship a challenge.

Wendy passed away in August 2001. Peter and Karen flew out to attend her funeral. Four weeks later, on September 11, 2001, one of Peter and John's good friends and classmates from Davidson also lost his life, leaping from a window before one of the Twin Towers collapsed.

Wendy's funeral was the last time Peter had spoken with John before yesterday's phone call.

Peter's plane landed on time in Albuquerque on Friday morning. He checked the notepad app on his phone, a memory tool that had become indispensable to him, to make sure he would go to the right rental car counter to meet John upon arrival. John had asked him to meet at the airport instead of taking a cab to his home so that they could depart as soon as Peter arrived.

Peter walked into the Budget rental car office and recognized John immediately. He was bent over near the vending machines, loading drinks into a tote bag. Peter walked briskly to his side, and when John rose, Peter threw his arms around him and just stood there for a moment, trying very hard not to cry.

John stepped back. The two men looked at each other and without having to say a word, they both knew the last twenty-five years of separation had somehow been instantly washed away. They smiled knowingly at each other, slapped each other on the back, and headed out to the car pickup lot.

"You have been taking care of yourself," said Peter. "You don't look a day over ninety."

John scoffed and replied, "And I see you have not lost your charm."

As they stepped into the lot, Peter quipped, "I hope you didn't get all frugal on me and rented something decent for me to drive."

John grinned. "Not to worry. I wasn't sure if you had porked out again like you did after graduation, so I got us a full-size hybrid SUV."

"I guess that means you are surprised to see what a great job I have done maintaining my girlish figure."

John laughed as they both threw their backpacks into the back seat of the car.

"So what's our first destination?" Peter asked John, pulling up the Waze app on his phone.

"I realize this last-minute trip was already a huge favor to ask of you, but I have another small favor to ask as well," John said. "Would you mind turning off your phone and letting this be an old-fashioned, device-free trip? I know the route to every place we are going and will happily serve as your guide. I actually left my own phone at home just in case someone should decide to track me with my phone's GPS signal."

Peter was surprised at hearing this, but he nodded at John's request. He was here to help John, after all.

"Excellent. We're going to Santa Fe first, and after that, we'll make our way over the next two days to Steamboat Springs."

———

As soon as they were on the road to Santa Fe, Peter began to ask the questions he hadn't had time to ask John during their call the night before.

"Would you mind telling me why you are so concerned about being tracked? And since I am also assuming you have not committed a crime, would you mind telling me who you think would be trying to find you?"

John reclined his seat a bit and then explained. "The who and the why are one in the same—my oldest daughter, Kate. I realize you have not seen her since Wendy's funeral, but to say she has grown up is a bit of an understatement." John chuckled. "Kate is now the senior partner in the same law firm I started when we moved to Albuquerque. That used to be my job. Quite simply, she is a force to be reckoned with. She is also the only one who knows I am having heath issues, and she is the one who bullied me into seeing a specialist when it became obvious that my headaches were getting worse."

John turned to Peter. "That reminds me. Since I am sure I'm going to be dealing with this headache issue a few times a day on this trip, I need to provide you some communications guidance. I have some pretty potent medication that I plan to take full advantage of, but the fact of the matter is I may need to just shut down for a little while and suffer."

Peter opened his mouth to reply but John held up his hand. "When this occurs, the answer to the question you will ask which will most likely be, 'Is there anything that I can do?' will be 'Yes, you can shut your mouth and let me suffer in peace.' To avoid this tender exchange between us, just try to ignore me. You will know the pain is under control again when I have the energy to engage once again in conversation. Now back to the question you asked concerning being tracked," John said, clearing his throat. "If my daughter knew about my diagnosis, she would drag me back into that hospital and ask them to pump every toxic chemical possible into my body, particularly if she thought it would give me a chance to stay alive for even just a few more weeks."

Here John paused, taking some time to collect his thoughts. "This all comes down to something very simple my friend. Regardless of what she may try to do, Kate is going to lose me, and she is not good at losing. I don't want her to also have to lose the battle over convincing me to undergo treatment. The only way I could make sure that does not happen is the path you and I are now on."

Peter responded in a quiet tone, and all he said was, "I understand."

The Sandia Mountains to the east of Albuquerque were now disappearing from sight in their rearview mirror.

It would be a short, one-hour drive to the base of the mountains surrounding Santa Fe. A few minutes later, John appeared to have had his first headache attack of the journey, closing his eyes and leaning his head against the window.

Eventually, he signaled he was recovered and that they could resume their conversation by informing Peter that he drove like an old lady.

"So, counselor," said Peter. "If you don't mind my asking, what did you do with your life after Wendy died? I do remember trying to call you a couple of times after the funeral, but you never called me back. I probably gave up too easily, but I figured you would reach out to me again when you were ready. I can honestly say I didn't think that call would happen twenty-five years later."

"I guess it was not until last night that I was ready to make that call," John replied after a moment. "If you don't mind, I don't really feel like talking about me right now. There are, however, a number of important subjects I would like to discuss with you during this trip, since it will be my last chance to do so. I am hopeful that you have not lost your ability to debate—and, of course, to lose most of those debates gracefully. I also really need someone to convince me that my predictions for the future should not be so bleak."

Peter chuckled and nodded. "No problem, my friend. I will do my best to respond to any questions you might have. That is, as long as I don't forget what the question was two minutes after you ask it."

"While I am delighted you brought your sense of humor with you on this trip, I do want to understand a little bit more about your own diagnosis," John said. "I would also appreciate it if you wouldn't sugarcoat it for me. I told you on my call the truth about my cancer diagnosis. Quid pro quo, Peter. This is a no bullshit trip."

The smile dropped from Peter's face. "I have what is called small vessel disease, which causes vascular dementia. This is the same disease that eventually killed my father ten years ago. It's not like your typical Alzheimer's, with a long and quiet journey into forgetting everything and everyone. It frequently adds personality alterations to the memory loss." Peter sighed heavily. "My father lived for two years after his diagnosis. The worst part was that he also became angry and sometimes violent. I had him moved to a facility in northern Virginia during those final years, and I was his only visitor during the last year of his life. None of my siblings or children could handle the visits anymore. It was like sitting in the room with a crazy guy screaming obscenities. When he finished performing for his visitors, he just sat there, moving his head from side to side. This is one of the reasons I am here, John," he said, looking at his friend from the corner of his eye to gauge his reaction. "When you told me what you were doing and why, I completely understood. Watching someone you love suffer for weeks or months and then die anyway is cruel for everyone. Watching someone you love die, in effect, when their memory goes, then die again physically , might be even crueler."

"I am really sorry, Peter. You know I love you like a brother and always have," John said softly. "I hope you'll forgive me for not digging deeper into your health issues during my call last night. As much as I wanted you to join me on my last trip to the mountains. I wouldn't have wanted you to risk your own health or safety in the process."

"There is nothing to forgive, John. My life has been on a downward spiral ever since those planes hit the towers in New York. Believe it or not, this is the first time in a long while that I feel like I am actually doing something that matters. I am honored you chose me for this trip and am looking forward to making up for lost time with the man who has been my best friend, whether he knew it or not, for my entire adult life."

"The feeling is mutual," said John with a smile. "I suggest that we go ahead and catch up on the family stuff, and then we can dive into a deeper conversation over lunch today. In my job as an attorney and in my life as a supportive father, I have always had to be careful what I say. Since today is the first day of the end of my life, I want to hash out with my best friend some of the things I have kept inside me for far too long."

"That is pretty ironic," Peter said, chuckling. "When I got off the plane this morning, I had to stop and close my eyes for a moment. It's difficult to explain, but I felt this rush come over my whole body. When I saw you, I suddenly understood what it was. Best friends play an important and unique role in people's lives. They allow you to talk about things you are not comfortable discussing with other people. I suddenly realized that I too have a lot of things that I want to hash out on this trip, particularly since I am now in the company of the master of dialogue and debate."

They spent the next half hour catching up on what the members of their families were doing and verbally introduced their grandchildren to each other. This conversation lasted until they arrived in Santa Fe.

John's dining selection took them off the highway and into the spacious dirt parking lot of a Mexican restaurant. It appeared to be mostly a takeout joint for travelers. The area behind the restaurant, however, had lots of old tables and beat-up chairs scattered about for those who wished to enjoy their carryout meal outdoors prior to returning to the road.

Peter and John placed their orders, took turns using the restroom, and then strolled outside to the back of the restaurant with their meals on trays. They sat at a small table nestled under a tree near the back fence.

After taking a few bites of his burrito, John set it back down onto the paper plate, wiped his mouth, and then began what would turn out to be the first of more than one discussion he had planned for the trip.

"So, Peter, let us take on our first important road trip conversation. While I finish this delicious burrito, I will be making the case for why mankind is completely fucked."

Peter gestured that John had the floor.

"As you know, I was a history major, and as such, I want to begin by making the case that the guy who came up with the story of the Four Horsemen of the Apocalypse was an idiot. I mean, first of all, two of the horsemen are totally redundant, and one of them is just a fact of life. Let us examine this for a moment. First you have War and Conquest. Those guys should be riding on the same horse. Do you know any conquests that were not the result of war? Do you know of any war that was not about conquest?"

Peter smiled but did not interrupt, knowing John was just beginning to get worked up.

"Now, let's take the guy on the horse that represents Death. As I am currently demonstrating, everyone dies. It is just part of life, not some bearded asshole charging at you with a spear. That leaves us with the only valid horseman of the Apocalypse, which is Famine. I think this guy was just a lucky guess. I mean, do you really think someone centuries ago had any idea that we would someday fry our planet like an egg and drive to extinction many of the fish and animals we eat? I am sorry, but no one is that prescient."

Peter recognized John's current pause as his invitation to join the conversation, so he did.

"Okay, so if you are committed to discrediting such a great cultural touchstone for so many bad movies and video games, then who would you vote to replace these four guys? I'm asking because I too had once given this topic some thought, and I will bet you that your Four Horsemen and mine are quite different."

John looked truly pleased and replied quickly. "Why don't you give me your Four Horsemen, since you have already wolfed down your lunch. Hopefully by the time you have finished, my burrito will be gone, and I can offer up my own candidates."

"That sounds fair. So my Four Horsemen are not what most people would think to be valid candidates, and before you jump in to tell me I am simply reflecting my bias from spending over forty years in the tech industry, I would ask you to hold your retort for a moment while I identify these four gentlemen and then explain why, in my view, they have positioned themselves to completely kick mankind's ass."

"My lips will remain sealed." Then, smiling, John added, "That is, of course, unless they are engaged in the consumption of food and drink."

Peter pushed his plate aside and continued. "Okay, so I am going to do these in chronological order. My horseman number one is the internet. For you nontechnical types, this began with the Department of Defense's ARPANET program in 1969. As a side note, I personally think it is pretty damn ironic that the Department of Defense would end up creating something that is so indefensible.

"The second of these gentlemen is actually a duo: the Smartphone and the Laptop. These two devices not only gave everyone in the world portable access to the internet, but today, they are a hundred times more powerful than the refrigerator-size computers I was selling to Uncle Sam forty years ago.

"This brings me to horseman number three, and that is Social Media. This guy is far too fucked up for me to refer to him as a gentleman.

"My final horseman is the glue that brings this technology team together. This guy is the new leader of the pack. As you probably already guessed, horseman number four is AI. In my view, it should be renamed IA for incoming apocalypse. Trust me, this guy is truly the final piece to our tech-driven demise."

John held his finger up to secure a moment of silence while he swallowed the last bite of his burrito.

"Well done, Peter. I find your logic to be quite sound, and I will in no way argue the eventual devastating impact that these technologies will most likely have. I like that you have recognized that, as they say, 'teamwork makes the dream work.' These guys are not all that lethal alone, but together, they are a true monster. I would like to suggest, however, that there are four other horsemen who, with the help of your tech team, will prove to be the real source of mankind's destruction. Let's think of your horsemen as the horses being ridden, but my guys will actually be pulling the triggers."

"By all means, please continue, counselor," Peter replied, a smile on his face.

"Okay, well, first I need to admit that I have always been addicted to watching *A Christmas Carol* every year on Christmas Eve. My favorite version is the one in which George C. Scott plays Scrooge. In the final part of the scene where he is visited by the Ghost of Christmas Present, Scrooge points to something hidden behind the ghost's long coat. As the ghost opens his coat, we are looking at two skinny, terrified children—one a boy, the other a girl. The ghost introduces them as mankind's children and tells Scrooge the following: 'This boy is Ignorance. This girl is Want. Beware them both, and all of their degree, but most of all beware this boy, for on his brow I see that written which is Doom, unless the writing be erased.'

"Ironically, the universal access to all knowledge that the internet should have made possible has not eradicated the ignorance this boy represents; it has made knowledge almost unattainable by destroying our ability to know what is the truth. As a result, I would suggest that mankind is getting progressively more ignorant," John said, shaking his head. "I am therefore borrowing my first horseman from Charles Dickens. His name is Ignorance. In order to secure and maintain power these days, you need to make sure that most people have no idea what is truly happening in the world and how and why it affects them. You need to recreate history in a way that supports your message. You need to feed people a daily dose of lies topped with a big scoop of blame. Honest to God, I fear that soon it will literally be impossible to know if what appears on your screen when you do a search is the truth or just something being fed to you to make sure you vote a certain way or become willing to look the other way when your country starts doing some really bad things. I mean, why do you think these guys tore down the Department of Education and are actively reengineering what kids learn? By my definition, ignorance does not mean you don't know anything. Ignorance means you don't know the truth.

"As far as your horseman Social Media goes, I believe he is actually a digital plague that is infecting the world with a global epidemic of narcissism. Narcissism happens to be my second horseman. Forget all that bullshit about learning to love yourself. You and I both grew up knowing we were pretty good students and athletes, but we did not obsess over it. After we graduated from college, we spent the rest of our lives living for and caring for our wives, our children, our friends, our clients, and our coworkers—and in your case, for the security of our nation," John said, gesturing at Peter.

"That way of living is dying my friend. Twenty-four hours a day, our young people are being bombarded with images telling them to focus on themselves. They need to look cool; they need to find a way to get rich and be able to show the world just how great they are. They need to be on social media, looking as badass as the dozens of influencers they follow like sheep.

"I also contend that the 'we' that had been America is gone. The majority of today's Americans care mostly about themselves, and I see no way to change this. Fascism and cults are back in style because the new dictators have learned how to manipulate all of these fragile but hungry egos. A divided nation and a nonstop social media war between the good guys and the bad guys feeds this chronic narcissism. It allows racists and misogynists to feel good about themselves because they think they are part of the winning team.

"I doubt anyone remembers John F. Kennedy's inaugural speech where he said, 'Ask not what your country can do for you—ask what you can do for your country.' Anyone who said this today would be immediately categorized as a woke, left-wing loser.

"Well, I guess I have beaten my horseman Narcissism nearly to death. Let's move on to my third horseman. This horseman was also introduced to me by my friend Charles Dickens. That little girl under the ghost's cloak that I mentioned before, her name was Want. This is a somewhat dated term, but its meaning at the time—as I am sure an English major like yourself knows quite well—was not having the basic necessities of life. Want meant hunger and the lack of shelter, clothing, and care. Want meant poverty.

"So, while poverty is a sad thing, you might still ask yourself, what is it about poverty that makes it scary? That answer is simple. If your children were hungry, what would you not do to feed them? Would you rob a local store? Would you steal from someone's garden? Would you wade across what is left of a nearly dry Rio Grande to find work in America's fields or in a chicken-processing plant?

"Want drives people to do these things. And, by the way, people who have everything they need are also plagued by want. Their want, however, is for a vacation house, a bigger boat, and an even better life than they already have. Many of these lucky people also do not want to live in a world where they have to worry about poverty and the problems it causes.

"With the current trajectory of income inequality in our country and the growth of want driven by a heartless political agenda favoring the rich, this horseman is coming by the millions, and it is scaring a lot of people. My third horseman, Want, also has another role to play. He is helping to fuel horseman number four. His name is Hatred.

"Let's jump ahead a few decades to when climate change has turned much of Mexico and Central America into a desert, along with half of the farms in California and the Southern states. Fortunately, the American population has been shrinking, but not fast enough to deal with the food shortages that have been created.

So the question is, how will we stop the millions of people now trying to push north across our borders out of sheer want? This is where Hatred comes in. Hatred allows you to demonize these poor people and make you see them as a threat to your very existence. It will allow you to put weapons on your border and to use them, because after all, these demons are going to murder, rape, and rob your family, as your AI-driven social media feed has now falsely depicted to you time and time again. They are coming for us so we must destroy them. The beginning of the end is when we are willing to kill people by the millions so they do not take what the more fortunate have."

John sighed then, lowering his head for a moment. Then he picked up his soda, took a drink, and continued. "So, Peter, these are my horsemen: Ignorance, Narcissism, Want, and Hatred. Your technology horses have helped to empower them, but in the end, it will be ignorant, selfish people with hearts pumped full of hatred who will be pulling the triggers and killing helpless and needy people by the millions.

"To end this rather depressing conversation with a touch of irony, I would also like to declare the biggest oxymoron of all time to be the word *mankind*. You, my friend, are kind. I am also very kind. But we are no longer in the majority. Man is simply no longer kind."

Peter just looked at John and shook his head, taking some time before replying. "I am very sorry to say that you have probably won your case, counselor. However, I would appreciate it if later in this trip and before you kick the bucket, you would be willing to discuss with me how this pending Armageddon might be avoided. As you might remember, I have always lived my life as a glass-half-full kind of guy. I would really like to find a way for the drink pitcher you are sending my way to not be filled with arsenic."

John chuckled. "Okay, let's make saving the world from its current path of destruction our primary dinner conversation topic for tonight. That should go well with a nice steak and a beer."

They got back into the car after John had filled his thermal bag with ice to cool their drinks for the afternoon's ride.

Telluride was about a six-hour drive from Santa Fe. This was to be the first of two planned overnight stays. They would also be breaking up the drive with a stop in Durango for an early dinner. Peter was tired from his early-morning flight and had picked up a couple of high energy drinks to help keep him alert. He was pleased to have discovered that being with John was a much-needed memory tonic for him. Before leaving, he had been concerned he would forget things that were important not to forget when driving, such as stopping at red lights. This had already led to a small fender bender two weeks earlier and caused his son, Scott, to demand that he stop driving immediately.

Highway 84 to Colorado

John loved this route. He had driven it dozens of times over the years, and yet it never got old for him.

The road was sandwiched between the Santa Fe National Forest to the west and the Carson National Forest to the east. Along the way, they would pass by both the Apache and Ute Nation reservations.

The last time he had made this trip was the year before Wendy died. It had been the final time his and Peter's families had met for their annual ski vacation. John and his family would often head out early and stop in Telluride for a couple of days of skiing before meeting up with Peter's family, who flew into the small airport just west of Steamboat Springs. John's wife and two daughters loved to ski and always looked forward to this annual vacation with great anticipation. John's oldest daughter, Kate, had become an accomplished skier at a very early age but chose not to pursue it as a competitive sport only because she loved playing basketball even more. Kelly, John's younger daughter, was also an excellent skier, but skied more for the joy and the beauty of the sport.

The mountains and the forests in north central New Mexico were a stark contrast to the rest of the state. The last hour or so before crossing the Colorado border included few man-made distractions to take John's eyes off the natural beauty surrounding him. John had always found this area to be a welcome change from living in Albuquerque, a city of earth tones—made browner still by local water conservation rules that discouraged traditional grass lawns and encouraged xeriscaping.

Both men had been quiet for the first part of the drive, mostly because John's medication was taking longer than anticipated to provide him relief from his pain. Fortunately, the relief these pills provided was lasting for several hours. This gave John time to either rest or to renew his conversations with Peter.

John knew that their lunch discussion had made it clear to Peter that John really did have a lot of things bottled up inside of him that he needed to discuss with someone who would not just listen but engage in discussion with him. Peter was his driver, yes, but he would also be the jury and the judge as John litigated his final case against the world.

John broke the silence about an hour north of Santa Fe.

"In an attempt to keep you from either overdosing on those caffeine cans you are drinking, or stopping every hour to take a piss, why don't you entertain me by telling me what you have really been up to for the last twenty-five years."

"I would be happy to do that. However, I will need to keep it pretty high level," Peter replied. "Since you now know about my memory problems, I will do the best I can to stay focused, but don't be surprised if I occasionally need to ask you who you are and where the hell we're going."

John laughed. "Not a problem. If you get confused, I will direct you to the things that I am most interested in. The first one is what happened after 9/11. I called you that day and left you a message because I knew that you and your company did work at the Pentagon and that your daughter was in school in New York City.

Peter just shook his head, frowned, and said, "I am sorry. I have no excuse for that. But if it makes you feel any better, I didn't return the calls from my parents or my two sisters either. Karen was the one who got ahold of my family and let them know we were all right."

"So what happened to you?"

"Three days after the attack, I got a call from the CEO of our company," Peter began. "He told me he had received a call from the FBI director's office asking for our technical help in identifying other potential terrorists who might have purchased airline tickets recently. As you recall, all flights were immediately grounded after the attack. Since I was running our government division and was the only executive with top secret security clearances, I was tasked with responding to this request, and needless to say, the response had to be immediate."

Here, Peter paused for a moment before continuing. John didn't quite know if he was gathering his thoughts or trying to remember what they'd been talking about. But then Peter continued with his explanation.

"Before continuing this story, however, I need to give you some context as to why our company got this call. One of our most successful software products at that time was a very sophisticated analytics tool kit that could perform complex queries on very large and diverse databases. Today, anyone can use Google or ChatGPT to do these kinds of queries for free, but twenty-five years ago, our company was pioneering this and helping other companies build their own server farms the size of a football field to power and host the massive amount of data required to perform this data analysis."

He smiled at John then, and John could see the pride Peter still had in the systems his teams had built over his career.

"I can give you an example of this that was directly related to 9/11. Walmart was, at the time, the nation's largest and fastest-growing retailer—and one of our biggest customers. Obviously, Amazon has kicked them off that pedestal since then. Anyway, a couple of weeks after the attack, the *Wall Street Journal* ran an article answering the question: How did Walmart corner the market for bottled water and American flags after 9/11? Without identifying our software and systems by name, the article described Walmart's state-of-the-art 'decision support system,' which was the backbone of their supply chain management.

"To keep from boring you with technical crap—which I am unfortunately really good at doing—here is what happened. The day of and the day after the attacks, while every buyer for every major retailer nationwide was at home glued to their TV sets, Our Walmart system was watching bottled water and American flags, among other things, flying off their shelves nationwide. Their computer system, with the help of our software, not only saw this happening but was programmed to respond by directly placing orders with their suppliers. When one supplier ran out of flags, it automatically pushed out orders to the second- and then the third-largest flag manufacturers to meet that demand. By the time the buyers from other retailers began to place their orders for flags, there were none to be had. Every American flag available was either in a Walmart store or in a Walmart warehouse, ready to replace the millions now being purchased," Peter said, looking over at John to make sure he was following. John nodded for him to continue.

"The request from the FBI director for our help was based on the fact that most of the major airlines were using our analytics software. With our help, they were able to identify the names of the terrorists on those planes and begin searching for others.

"That first mission blossomed over time to dozens of other missions as the government scrambled to keep this tragedy from happening again. The new Department of Homeland Security used our systems and software as the foundation for much of their early work.

"But, as governments often do, ours decided not just to protect our country from further terrorist attacks but to exact revenge on the homes of our new enemies. As a result, new offensive, classified programs began popping up like wildflowers, and our systems became an integral part of that process. It was not hard to get support from my company's CEO to double the size of our government division almost overnight. None of us could tell him specifics, but he was happy to give us both the technical and staffing support that we needed as long as the government funding continued to flow, and trust me, it was flowing like a waterfall."

Peter heaved a great, long sigh. "So, while my wife and children sat at home, worrying like everyone else in our country in the weeks and months that followed, instead of being there to comfort them, I disappeared down a rabbit hole that I would not find my way out of for almost fifteen years. This was not just the beginning of the end of my marriage; it was the beginning of the end of who I was. That funny and incredibly charming young man you met that summer at Davidson College was gone. What replaced him was a relentless techno-warrior who was trying to become something he had always wanted to be."

In the pause that followed, John asked, "And what, might I ask, had you always wanted to be?"

"A hero, of course. Might I continue now, counselor? I would like to try to provide you with my defense for the crime of going AWOL from the ones I love."

"Of course," said John.

"As a kid with an active imagination, and growing up in the sixties, I dreamed all the time about becoming a hero. In elementary school, during the weekends, you could always find me and my friends dressed up in World War II army uniforms with plastic helmets and tommy guns, fighting heroic battles against imaginary Nazis. There was a drive-in theater not far from our home that also fed us the latest Western heroics of John Wayne and Henry Fonda. As I got older, 007 arrived on the screen. In the sixth grade, for Christmas, my parents got me a toy James Bond briefcase with a handgun inside that could shoot plastic bullets through a hole in the case. I thought I had died and gone to heaven," Peter said, chuckling at the memory of his younger self.

"In high school, with my baby fat slipping away, I went out for football, wrestling, and track. Once again, these were opportunities for heroics, though of a different kind. I probably would have been crazy enough to sign up to go to Vietnam if it was not for my football scholarship and the fact that I had fallen in love with the game."

Peter paused for a moment to take a sip from his energy drink, and John used this as an opportunity to enter the conversation.

"Thank you, Mr. Grove, for your testimony today. But now, I would like to begin my cross-examination."

Peter smiled. "By all means, counselor."

"First, while I completely understand and appreciate your heroic quest, I find it a less than compelling excuse for your transgressions later in life. I, as you might remember from our joint birthday parties in college, was born just two weeks before you and trust me, us Midwestern boys fought just as many imaginary Nazis as you did, and we also lived for the next Western or spy movie to come out.

"My case against your excuse for your extended disappearing act is based on the fact that I knew you so well the first time you had the opportunity to go down a national security mission rabbit hole—but you did not."

Peter nodded and motioned for John to continue.

"As I recall, in the early eighties, you were working as an executive selling computers to the intelligence community. Ronald Reagan was in office, and the Cold War was still pretty scary. I also remember you joking on the chairlift about how you had almost failed your first CIA polygraph because of your more-than-occasional hit on the bong our senior year. We were best friends in the eighties and yet your covert global trips and your company's focus on helping to end the Cold War never got in the way of your kids sporting events or our family vacations.

"So, Mr. Grove, I would like you to please explain to the jury why you maintained a reasonable work-life balance while helping to battle the threat of global nuclear war and yet you decided to desert, both physically and emotionally, everyone you loved after 9/11."

Peter glanced over at John and shook his head ruefully. "I missed you, my friend."

Then he sighed once again and said, "My first defense for this rather extreme difference in behavior is based on two things. The first was the difference between the Soviet threat in the eighties and the terrorist threat. While Ronald Reagan was not my favorite president, he came to office with a commitment to ending the Cold War, and his defense team came up with what turned out to be a highly classified yet ultimately winning strategy.

"By the early eighties, the Soviets were going broke. The cost of matching our nuclear arsenal and our global spy networks was skyrocketing. Reagan's plan was simple but effective. He decided to bankrupt them by ratcheting up the cost of maintaining the balance of power.

"Reagan's team trumpeted the Star Wars program and started feeding known Russian agents fake intelligence that we had expanded our arsenal and built several covert command centers nationwide that could survive a first nuclear strike and allow us to retaliate. Ironically, on November 9, 1989, 11/9, not 9/11, the year after Reagan left office, the Berlin Wall came down, and the Cold War was over."

Peter held up a finger. "So here is the direct answer to your question. Those of us engaged in this almost decade-long campaign of deception all knew that the Russian bear was mortally wounded and that the end was near. The role my team played in equipping satellite ground stations and both real and fake command centers was not really that pivotal. I could feel good about the work we were doing without worrying about skyscrapers and airplanes crashing to the ground.

"My second defense for my actions is skyscrapers and airplanes crashing to the ground."

John nodded, beginning to see where Peter's argument was going.

"The war on terrorism began that day, and we lost the first battle. The role my team was asked to play was pivotal to making sure we did not lose again. We needed to quickly adapt our technology to take on missions that were never envisioned by our developers. We needed to make our systems more portable so that we could stay off the internet. Long days stretched into weeks, weeks into months, and months into years.

"As far as my family goes, my two kids were in college during 9/11 and needed me less. My wife eventually grew tired of living alone most of the time and gave up on me. This made it even easier for me to bury myself in my work. I didn't even have a dog anymore, because he left with her."

Peter cleared something from his throat before continuing. "I tell you this without seeking either admiration or sympathy. I lost my balance, and with it, I lost everything I loved. My addiction to heroics and being brought up on stories of the sacrifices that heroes must make drove me night and day for a very long time.

"When I finally walked away, I discovered I was not a hero after all—I was just alone. I had pissed away a big part of my life and in the end, I cannot tell you for certain if we actually saved any American lives. I can tell you, however, with great certainty, that we helped take away tens of thousands of lives in other countries. Lives of not just men but women and children whose only crime was living in the wrong place during our 9/11 revenge campaign," he said, shaking his head. "That is all I have to say on this topic, counselor. I throw myself on the mercy of the court."

John looked closely at Peter's face and sighed. "Okay, my friend, court is adjourned. It appears you created your own prison and have already served a long enough sentence. Would you mind telling me what finally ended this obsession and what you did when it was over?"

"The end was anticlimactic. Eventually, new technology and software simply made us obsolete. The company was sold to a competitor, and I was allowed to retire rather than be laid off like so many of the people who had worked with me. I had more money than I needed, and my two kids both had busy lives and had gotten used to never seeing me. I took up hiking, which was a great sport for a lonely old man with a lot of time on his hands and no one to spend it with. I also recently started to donate to and volunteer at a local animal rescue center. These new animal friends became my first attempt to fill the very large empty spot in my heart."

Peter took a moment to finish his drink and then added softly, "I want you to know that I thought about calling you many times but was too embarrassed. I had watched you do everything that could be done to keep your wife alive and saw at the funeral what her loss had done to you. Meanwhile, I lost the only woman I have ever loved by simply deserting her."

John put his hand on Peter's shoulder and said quietly, "There is nothing to forgive." Then he paused for a moment. "You know, in hindsight, you really should have gone down the entrepreneurial career path you envisioned.. After all, you had that great moneymaking idea you told me about on one of our first ski trips.

"What are you talking about?" Peter asked, glancing over at him.

"Come on," said John. "Don't tell me you don't remember the product idea you came up with when you heard that Pope John Paul II was going to visit America that summer."

Peter broke into laughter.

"Of course I do," he said, once he'd caught his breath. "I was going to launch a personal care product for Catholics called "Pope Soap on a Rope". The slogan was simple. Every time you stepped into the shower and grabbed your molded Pope-shaped bar dangling from a rope, you'd be able to 'wash away more than just your sins.'"

"You see! You missed the opportunity to avoid all that pain by going down the wrong career path," John said, chuckling. Then he added, "I do have another question to ask you, however. So far, I have not seen any real indication in your words or actions that you have dementia. I mean, you remembered 'Pope Soap on a Rope' quickly enough. Do you mind sharing with me a bit more about your cognitive issues?"

"Well, unfortunately, I do not have the classic case of Alzheimer's disease or dementia, where you just start to forget things until you eventually forget everything—that is, of course, if you don't die first," Peter replied. "My version began with forgetting next-moment things. For example, I would decide to get up and walk into my kitchen to get a drink. Once I stood up, I had to stop for a moment to try to remember why I was standing. I would walk to the mailbox to mail a letter on the way to getting a morning coffee and when I got home the only way that I knew that I had mailed it was the fact that it was no longer in my pocket. I had no memory of actually placing it in the box less than an hour later.

"Eventually, this started to happen with the capture of certain words I want to say in the middle of a conversation. I began to hesitate and grope around for the word I lost. Sometimes it is the name of a local restaurant or a person whose name I should know. I compensate by trying to pick another word immediately available to me to cover this up, but my conversation becomes broken with these unusual and uncomfortable moments of hesitation."

"I see," said John.

"This has been getting much worse, and it is now being accompanied by the traditional loss of long-term memories. Seeing you again, I have been doing better with the memories of our time together, but that is because you are here. Without something or someone physical to help me to find a memory, it is now often simply gone. I could give you dozens of examples in the last few days alone. Seeing a photo of my favorite actress and forgetting her name. Remembering the story in a novel I just read, but not the name of the novel or the author.

"My verbal interactions with almost everyone these days—except for my son Scott, who is the only person aware of my diagnosis—have become perfunctory. I offer short, casual greetings, and I avoid real conversations now like the plague. You, my friend, are an exception to this rule," Peter said, turning to look at John for a moment before returning his eyes to the road. "Unless I start to stutter or drool, I want to take advantage of our time together to the maximum degree possible. If my verbal skills aren't as sharp as they used to be, I don't care. I need to get some things off my chest just as badly as you do. So if there is an occasional pause or request for assistance, your patience and help will be much appreciated."

John looked over at Peter and said, "I am grateful you joined me on this trip. You know I treasure your friendship, and so I will be happy to cross your t's and dot your i's if you need help. I can almost always tell what is in your heart, so if what comes out of your mouth has become a little disjointed, it's no big deal."

"Thank you," Peter said, smiling.

"Can you do me a favor, though, and pull off at the next rest stop so we can sit outside for a while? I need a break after my last brain attack."

Rest Stop, Highway 84

The farther north they traveled, the more the August heat of New Mexico began to surrender to the coolness of the mountains. The final rest stop before the Colorado border was weathered but nice. As they got out of the car, a breeze welcomed them. Peter headed to the restroom, while John strolled along a trail that led to a shaded park with a number of worn benches sitting empty. Theirs was the only car in the lot. Tourist season had come to an end, with kids going back to school soon. John picked out a bench with a good view of the mountains and swallowed another pill. He was thinking about his two daughters. His younger daughter, Kelly, was married, had two young children, and lived a very busy life. While she made plenty of room for him in their lives, after they moved to Portland, it had been difficult for John to see them regularly.

His relationship with her older sister, Kate, was very different.

Kate had been the one to help him through the death of her mother. From the beginning of her illness until the end, he knew that as hard as he had tried, it had been her, not John, who had been the rock the family had leaned on.

John and Kate had had a special relationship since she was a small child. She was smart, curious, and had a bundle of energy. Unlike her sister, who was happy with her toys and books, Kate loved to be outside and in motion every chance she got. She was an athlete and a risk-taker. She'd also known very early in life exactly who she was and who she wanted to be. While her basketball skills helped to get her into Harvard, it was her keen mind and work ethic that carried her through their law school.

When she graduated from law school, she worked for four years in the Albuquerque district attorney's office but eventually found her way to her father's practice. Within a few years, she was taking on and winning some of the firm's most important cases. Eventually, John came to the realization that while he was a successful attorney in his own right, Kate was now the true star of their practice.

Kate had told her father after graduation that she had no plans to ever get married and that this was simply a lifestyle choice she had made. She also made it clear she had no interest in discussing or debating this decision. She had several good friends, mostly from college and law school, with whom she kept in touch, but as far as anyone knew, she rarely dated. She was tall and very attractive but made it clear to both her male and female friends that she had no interest in a romantic relationship. She loved her family, her friends, her work, and her dogs, and that was enough for her.

Kate always had a dog. Each time her current dog passed away, she would go to the local animal shelter and pick an older dog no one would want. She would bring them home and give them her love and the best medical care possible until they too passed away of old age a few years later. The next day, she would be back at the shelter picking out her next canine companion.

John knew Kate didn't really need him anymore—if she ever had. All Kate needed was to be able to fight for her clients and for those she loved. John was certain she would never forgive him for not giving her the chance to fight to keep him alive.

Peter strolled over to the bench with two sodas from the vending machine and sat down next to John, handing him one.

"Sorry," he said, "they didn't have Mountain Dew, so you are stuck with a Dr. Pepper."

John held his can high and replied, "Just think, if we had not gone to school in North Carolina, we might never have become addicted to these redneck Pepsi products."

Peter took a sip from his drink. "So do you feel up to a quid pro quo, counselor? I would love to hear what you were doing during the first quarter of this century.

John took a pull from his drink before he began. "Let me start at what I consider to be the end. The life I wanted and planned to live died along with Wendy. If you thought I was bad at the funeral, you have no idea how bad I was in the days and weeks that followed. The girls were away at college, and every friend I had in Albuquerque who did not work in our practice was a husband of one of Wendy's almost endless network of women friends. When she died, despite how much several of those husbands tried, those friendships soon died as well. We had been a network of couples, and I was now a single. It also probably did not help that I had no desire to be constantly reminded in social contexts of my loss.

"I chose, like you, to throw myself into my work. For the next decade, that is what I did—I worked. I did not golf or date or even go out to dinner, unless it was with my daughters. To help deal with my anger, I took up boxing for old dudes and became a gym rat in the spare time that I allowed myself. I built my law firm from six to over twenty attorneys, and we, I am proud to say, won a lot more cases than we lost.

"My life finally became bearable again when Kate joined the firm," John said, smiling. "For the first time in my life, every day, I was working with someone I loved very much. I began to enjoy my work more, but what I really enjoyed was helping Kate become something she was destined to be—a great lawyer.

"A few years ago, I finally gave in and took up golf again. I developed a few golf buddies who were satisfied with seeing me only at the club, and I settled into my new life, trying very hard not to be angry at the world every day for what had been taken from me."

He was silent for a few moments, and Peter let him be.

Eventually, he continued. "I now realize you were the last best friend I ever had, and that is the reason I called you last night and asked for your help. I have spent the last twenty-five years working and never made any effort to let anyone new into my life. I feel like I have been a good father and grandfather, all things considered, but there was no room left in my heart for anyone new after Wendy died.

"That, my friend, is how I have spent my time in the twenty-first century. I hope you will excuse me now while I take a piss."

Peter nodded, absorbing what he'd shared and said simply, "I'll meet you back at the car."

Albuquerque

It was almost midnight on Friday when Kate finally left the office. She probably would have stayed later, but she had to get home to walk and feed her dog, Roscoe. He was a three-legged, nine-year-old mutt who had won the adoption lottery when she'd selected him from the animal shelter. After just one year with Kate, he had gone from timid to one of the friendliest and most beloved animals at the local dog park.

Kate's townhouse was not far from her office, in an upscale, gentrified part of the city where she could easily walk to the gym, to the grocery store, and to the dog park, her three most common destinations other than her office and the courthouse. Her three-year-old SUV only had about six thousand miles on it.

She got up early Saturday and took Roscoe for his morning visit to the park, as was their routine. Afterward, she walked to the gym. Unlike many young women in her generation, Kate had grown up taking more pride in her athletic ability than in her appearance. Her mother and father had helped to promote this, but it had not been difficult for them. She was always happiest when she was pushing herself physically, whether on the basketball court, on the ski slope, or in the gym. The fact that she was very attractive made it difficult, however, for people to recognize her as the tomboy she was.

While she had dated off and on during high school and college, she had never had a relationship that lasted more than a few months. This was always her decision. Men who got too close and wanted too much eventually turned her off. She was happy with living her life as she had planned it and never felt as though she was missing anything by not committing to share it with one man forever.

After grabbing a coffee on the way home from the gym, she went back to her home office to resume work on the case that was her current top priority. She was defending a twenty-six-year-old woman who had been charged with manslaughter for killing her husband. It was a case that had received lots of press in Albuquerque, and not a small amount of political bias on social media. Her client was Hispanic and had been abused by her husband repeatedly. She had stabbed him with a kitchen knife in self-defense, cutting an artery. He bled to death before the ambulance arrived. The assault occurred when she came home from work and found him abusing their five-year-old daughter. Her husband was a white man, and his parents were wealthy and clearly looking for revenge for the loss of their only child. They were also seeking custody of their only granddaughter.

The state prosecutor handling the case was someone she knew quite well. He was very ambitious, and she was certain the only reason her client had been charged at all, considering her recorded history as an abuse victim, was the fact that her skin was brown. Kate was working very hard to make certain this young woman and her daughter did not suffer any more than they already had.

Around lunchtime, she took a break and called her father to see how he was doing. She was surprised when her call went straight to voicemail, but she assumed he was on the golf course, where ringing phones were frowned upon. She headed to the grocery store to pick up a few things. While walking down one of the aisles, she spotted Dr. Martin, the doctor her father had met with at her insistence when his headaches first started. He waved to her and pushed his cart toward her.

"Kate, it's nice to see you again. Have you spoken with your father about his visit this week?

Taken aback, Kate said, "No, I was not aware he had a visit with you this week."

The doctor shifted on his feet uncomfortably. "I'm sorry. He told me he would be discussing his diagnosis and recommended treatments with his family, and I just assumed he meant as soon as he got home."

"He has told me nothing," she said tightly. "Perhaps you would be so kind as to share with me the diagnosis and treatment you are referring to."

The doctor hung his head a little and replied sheepishly. "I really cannot discuss this information with you for patient privacy reasons. As an attorney, I'm sure you understand this. Why don't you just call him and explain that we met by accident today, then let him fill you in?"

"Sure, thanks," Kate said curtly. She immediately turned around, left her cart in the aisle without checking out, and walked quickly to her car. She drove out of the parking lot and headed straight to her father's house. On the way, she tried to call him again several times but got no reply.

A few minutes later, she pulled into the circular driveway at the front of John's house. When she got to the front door, she was surprised to find it locked, something her father rarely did. She rang the doorbell, but her father did not come to the door. After several loud knocks and another ring, she gave up, digging out her spare key from her purse.

When she entered the house, it was dark and quiet.

"Dad?" she called out. No reply.

She went upstairs to check the primary bedroom, then out to the garage, and then came back inside to check his office. The office was as neat as a pin. She knew he had not gone to Santa Fe to play golf because his car was in the garage and so were his golf clubs. She took out her phone and called her father again, but this time she heard a vibrating sound coming from his desk drawer. She went to the desk, opened the top drawer, and was surprised to find his phone there. He always kept his phone with him.

This made no sense to her. After checking the house and garage again, she went back to his home office, sat down at his desk, and picked up his phone. She knew his password, so she had no problem checking his recent calls.

When she looked at his call records, she was surprised to see one of the last call he'd made had been late Thursday afternoon and was to his old college friend Peter Grove. She had not heard this name for a very long time, and she had no idea her father was still corresponding with him. What bothered her most was the fact that there were no other calls after that one. The phone's charge was just over 15 percent, and there were several missed calls listed, mostly from her. She opened his text messages and saw that he had apparently taken an Uber on Friday morning. The driver rating and tip request sent following the ride had gone unanswered, which made sense because he had left his phone behind.

Taking a few deep breaths, she steadied herself emotionally and started to try to figure out why he had not told her about his doctor's appointment on Thursday and why he had obviously lied about his weekend plans. Where had he gone in an Uber on Friday morning and why had he left his phone in the drawer of his desk?

The Uber receipt showed the destination of his last ride. It was the Albuquerque airport. If he had indeed gone to the airport without his phone, then he had to have been carrying with him the only credit card he ever used, which was his frequent flyer Visa card. She opened his phone's wallet app and clicked on his credit card. The last charge on the account was at the hospital pharmacy on Thursday.

Kate thought for a moment, then jumped out of her seat and went over to an old jewelry box on one of the bookshelves. She opened it and, as she suspected, found it empty. Her dad had always been a very generous man, and he always kept well over a thousand dollars in twenty-dollar bills in that box. If he was going to a business dinner or other social event, he liked to tip the people serving him in cash, as he knew every penny would remain with the person who parked his car or took his coat.

It was now obvious to Kate that wherever her father was, he did not want anyone to know his destination.

She began searching through his desk drawers to see if there were any other clues related to his sudden disappearance. She discovered the medical document from his visit that week in the same drawer where she had found his phone. She read it quickly and gasped at the longevity diagnosis of his clearly terminal disease.

There was no longer any mystery. Her father was going somewhere to commit suicide, and she had to find him.

Once she established in her own mind the facts of what was happening, she shifted immediately from feelings of fear and sadness to a state of unfettered focus and resolve.

She was not going to let her father die without her. She was going to find him, bring him back, and do everything humanly possible to keep him alive.

She sat back down and began looking through the rest of the apps on his phone for clues. After several minutes of searching unsuccessfully, she remembered the last call he made, to Peter Grove. Maybe he had contacted Peter and confided in him about his plans. After all, they had been best friends for many years.

She called Peter's number but got his voicemail, so she left him a message. Noticing her father's laptop was missing—he'd probably taken it with him—she decided to go back to her home office. She needed to get on her own computer and see what she could find. She also needed to charge his phone, as it was now her only potential source of clues to his whereabouts.

On the short drive back home, Kate tried as hard as she could to focus on the only thing that mattered to her now: Where had her father gone? She assumed he had taken a one-way flight somewhere, and purchased the ticket with cash, so her first search online needed to focus on finding out those details.

When she got home, she went straight to her office and sat down at her desk. She plugged her father's phone into her charging station and then tried to call Peter Grove once again. It went straight to voicemail for a second time, so it was likely his phone was dead or he had it turned off. She needed to reach Peter and needed to do so quickly. The call record had shown that John's call with Peter had lasted just over thirty minutes, so she was certain that whatever her father's plans were, he had shared them with Peter.

Just then, another name popped into her head: Scott Grove. Scott was Peter's oldest son. She and Scott had been good friends growing up, as they were the oldest kids and two best skiers in the two families. The last time she had seen him had been their last family ski vacation. He was sixteen at the time, and she eighteen, and in her first year at Harvard.

Kate began to search online using her favorite AI tool, which included links to social media sites. It did not take long for her to locate Scott in New York City. The first photo that popped up showed that while he had clearly aged, he was clean-shaven and had the same build and youthful face she remembered. A deeper search disclosed his position at a New York hedge fund, and there was another picture of him at a local charity road race. She used her firm's contact information software to find his address in New York and his phone number. Fortunately, he had not blocked this professional search tool, which was used almost exclusively by law firms in support of their cases.

She dialed his number and was surprised when he immediately answered the phone.

New York City

Scott Grove was walking back from the gym when his phone rang. He looked at the number and recognized the New Mexico area code. Since his spam filters hadn't stopped the incoming call, he decided to answer it. "Hello?"

"Scott, this is Kate Eastman calling. I don't know if you remember me, but we used to ski together when we were kids. I'm John Eastman's oldest daughter."

"Of course I remember you, Kate," Scott replied, surprised to hear from her. "As I recall, you almost got me killed several times when I tried to follow you through the trees at Steamboat."

Kate chuckled. "It was nothing personal, and as I recall, you returned the favor every chance you got. Now, for why I'm calling. I am sorry to disturb you, but I was wondering if you could help me get in touch with your father. I have his number, but he's not answering his phone."

"That's odd," said Scott. "He takes his phone everywhere with him, and he is a fanatic about returning voice messages promptly. What is this about? Is there anything I can help you with?"

"Yes. Would you mind putting me on hold while you call your dad to see if he answers your call? If he does, maybe you can add me to the call, and I can discuss my problem with both of you. It is about my father, and it's urgent that I speak with him."

Scott had been walking the Central Park route back to his apartment and decided to sit down on a nearby bench. "No problem. I can do that right now."

"Thank you so much," Kate replied.

Scott dialed his father's number and was surprised when it went straight to voicemail. He hung up on that call and took Kate off hold.

"My call went right to voicemail. When did you say you tried to call him?" Scott asked.

"Over an hour ago," replied Kate.

"That makes no sense," said Scott. "It's Saturday. He should be walking dogs from the local shelter or out for a walk or hike, and he never leaves his phone behind. He also always answers my calls."

"Scott, I think I better explain to you why it is so important for me to get in touch with your father," Kate said, her tone firm but worried. "My father is missing. No one has heard from him since Thursday night. My father never goes anywhere without his phone, but I found it in his desk drawer this morning. The last call he made was Thursday afternoon, to your father. Based on the call log, they talked for over thirty minutes. I am hoping your dad knows where my father is and could help me find him."

Scott hesitated for a moment before responding. "I am so sorry, Kate. Look, I'm only about five minutes from my apartment. Let me get to my computer and see if I can dig up the number for one of my dad's next-door neighbors. I will ask them to see if he's home. Maybe there is just a problem with his phone. Give me a few minutes and I will call you right back."

"Thank you so much for your help, Scott. I will be waiting for your call," said Kate.

Scott got off the bench and ran back to his apartment, on the lower east side of Central Park, where he lived alone. He rushed past the doorman with a quick wave and took the elevator to the twentieth floor. Once inside his apartment, he threw down his small gym bag, grabbed a water from the fridge, and went straight to his office. Like even the most upscale apartments in New York, the second bedroom that served as his office was small. The walls surrounding his desk, which looked out over the park through a large window, were covered with shelves full of books, memorabilia, photographs, and other signs of a busy and well-traveled life.

He logged on to his computer and opened the folder in which he kept his father's files and account information. He quickly found the number he was looking for. Jake Kensington and his wife were his father's next-door neighbors. They were in their late seventies and, unlike most of their neighbors, did not have a second home somewhere else. They were retired professors with no children and were usually at home this time of year. Scott was delighted when Jake answered his call.

"Mr. Kensington, this is Scott Grove calling. I was hoping you could do me a favor," he said.

"Scott, how are you? It's funny you should call. Your dad was supposed to be joining us for dinner last night but knocked on the door yesterday and said he had to take a rain check," said Jake.

"Really? Did he say why he had to cancel?"

"Why yes, he did," said Jake. "He said he had heard from an old friend of his from college who needed some help, and he was going to be heading out of town for a few days. I kidded him about whether he was back to doing secret tech stuff, but he just laughed and reminded me he was no longer in that business."

"Thanks," said Scott. "That explains why I haven't been able to reach him. Did he tell you where he was going and when?"

"No," said Jake. "He didn't, but Susan said she saw him getting into an Uber with his backpack early yesterday morning."

"Thanks, Jake. Have a good rest of your day," Scott said before hanging up.

He thought for a moment and then opened the file on his computer that held documents related to his role as his father's power of attorney, in case anything happened to him. One of those documents was a listing of all his father's online accounts and current passwords. He quickly wrote down the username and password for the credit card his father used the most. He went to their website and entered the log-in information.

Once he scrolled down the page, he saw the last charge his father had made had been on Thursday night. That charge was for a ticket on Southwest Airlines, which Peter used most often because he preferred flying out of Baltimore/Washington International Airport, a major Southwest hub.

Scott attempted to log in to his father's Southwest account using the password he had but was blocked by the site's security software because he was not on his father's laptop. The login software offered him a one-time code to gain access via text or email. Since he had no access to his father's phone, he chose email, then quickly opened another browser and logged in to his father's email account using the listed username and password. He breathed a sigh of relief when the site's security let him in. There, at the top of the list of unread emails, was the Southwest security email with an access code. He quickly switched browsers and entered the code, opening his father's frequent flyer account. He saw that he had taken a Southwest flight to Albuquerque on

Friday morning. He also noticed that there was no return flight listed.

Scott picked up the phone and called Kate. She answered on the first ring.

"Thanks for the call, Scott. Did you find out anything?"

"I found out that my father flew to Albuquerque on an early-morning flight yesterday. He did not book a return flight."

"Oh my god," said Kate. "Based on the Uber receipt ride I found on my father's phone, that must mean he went to the Albuquerque airport yesterday morning to meet your father."

Kate paused for a moment, and Scott heard her take a deep breath. "I know what is happening, but I have no idea where they are."

"I don't understand," said Scott.

"My father has gone somewhere with your father, and when he gets there, he is going to commit suicide."

Scott replied, his heart now racing, "I don't understand. Why do you think your father is going to commit suicide?"

"My father has cancer and just found out Thursday that it's terminal. The medical files suggest he probably has only about four months left to live, but with a heavy dose of radiation and chemo, he might be able to stretch it out to six months. He also did not tell me he was going to the hospital last Thursday and lied about where he was going to be this weekend. I wouldn't have found out about his diagnosis if I had not stopped by his house today."

At this point, she sounded close to tears. "I know what he is doing. He has decided he doesn't want to suffer through the same treatments my mother suffered through the year she died from cancer. I am also sure his main reason is that he doesn't want my sister and I to have to go through that agony all over again."

"Kate, I still don't understand," Scott said. "You two were always so close when we were kids. Why did he purposely hide his diagnosis from you, and why didn't he just confide in you about his intention to take his own life?"

"Because he knew I wouldn't let him do it," she said. "He knows I would do everything within my power to stop him. I would probably even have had him declared no longer capable of making this decision due to his illness, and as his power of attorney, I probably would force him into taking those treatments. I realize this makes me sound pretty heartless, but I'm not," she said, her voice cracking. "I love my father more than anyone on earth. I cannot let him kill himself. If there is a way to keep him alive, even a remote chance of remission, I need to convince him that this is what my sister and I want him to do. Physically, my dad is tough as nails for his age, and if anyone has the strength to fight this, it's him. I need to be there with him and to fight this thing, Scott. I have to find him before it's too late."

Then, Kate lost control of her emotions and burst into tears. Scott listened to her crying uncontrollably, repeating over and over again, "I can't let him die. I have to find him."

Scott found himself struggling to fight back his own tears. When her sobbing subsided, he said to her in a firm but comforting tone, "I promise you, Kate, I am going to do everything I can to help you find your father. But I need to take a moment to think about the best way to do that. There are a few things I need to check on. I promise I will call you back within the hour."

"Thank you," Kate said quietly, and then she hung up the phone.

In the Air

Scott had been lucky to catch the last flight to Albuquerque Saturday evening. The two-hour time difference would get him to the airport in New Mexico around 10 p.m. He'd told Kate on his last call to her that he would grab an Uber and meet her at her house. He packed a change of clothes in his leather backpack with the logo of his company on the flap and placed his laptop in the protective slot in the center of the bag.

Just before he left, Scott had called Kate to let her know he had discovered a charge on his father's credit card that'd been made Friday afternoon at a gas station north of Santa Fe. This clearly indicated that his father and John were not flying but driving to wherever they were going. He and Kate agreed that the best course of action was for him to bring his laptop and continue to see if there were any more charges when he arrived in Albuquerque. This would allow them to try to follow the trail of Peter's credit card transactions from the road.

Despite Kate's exhaustive search of her father's phone, she had found no correspondence that would provide any clues as to where he was headed. This meant they were now totally reliant on Peter's credit card data, as it was now also obvious that Peter had turned off his phone.

They planned to drive all night, taking turns at the wheel, hoping their fathers' journey involved at least a couple of hotel stops.

Kate was most worried about the fact that there had been no more charges after the one at the gas station yesterday afternoon and said to Scott that they might be too late. Scott provided her some comfort when he suggested that even if there was no motel receipt on Peter's charge card, she had said that her father was traveling with cash and he was most likely using that cash to pay for most of their travel expenses. Scott also reminded her that Peter will have to turn his phone back on at some point to make arrangements to return home. This meant that every hour Peter's phone remained turned off was another hour of hope. They agreed that the best plan was to head straight to that gas station where the receipt came from and check the credit card account every ten or fifteen minutes once they left her house.

It was a long flight and in anticipation of what would probably be a sleepless night, Scott tried to sleep on the plane but found that to be impossible. Instead, he put on his headphones, turned on a playlist, and pulled his sketch pad out of his bag.

Scott always carried his sketch pad with him when he traveled for business. It gave him comfort. During a high school art class, he'd discovered he had an artistic skill that was quite unusual. While he had never tried to draw or paint anything traditionally artistic, he somehow had the ability to look at anything—whether a person, a place, or a thing—and draw a sketch of what he saw that, when finished, would look like a photograph had just been taken.

The only people who knew about this skill were his family and a few close friends, and he had tried over the years to keep it that way. He had a lot of experience hiding things he thought might not fit his image, and besides, he'd had little time for drawing during college or graduate school. His career in the financial services industry had been even more demanding timewise, so he simply used the sketch pad as a way to pass the time on his travels or when he took a photo on his phone he found compelling enough to draw. While he was an avid reader, he did almost all his reading via audiobooks while he exercised or traveled.

Fortunately, the flight was a smooth one and did not disturb his drawing. A very old picture on his cell phone was his current subject. Drawing a likeness of it calmed him and allowed him to think clearly about the important task before him.

Most of his thoughts while on the flight were about his father. The rest were about Kate.

From the time he was a young boy, he had not just looked up to and loved his father, but he had tried as best he could to make Peter proud of him.

Scott had inherited his mother's hazel eyes and softer facial features, but his body was much like his father's. Although not as tall, Scott had the same broad shoulders and linebacker build. He worked out every day, and though in his early forties, he looked very much as he did in college—with the exception of the gray hair that was beginning to infiltrate its sandy-brown counterparts.

Scott had focused his thoughts on his father and his friendship with John in the hope he could come up with something that might help Kate to locate him.

He was aware of how close the two men had been while he was growing up, and even though that relationship had lapsed for over twenty years, he knew his father would never have turned down this request.

The thing that concerned him the most was his father's cognitive issues. He knew his dad had been playing down the signs of dementia that Scott had begun to notice on their calls and when they got together. He had also had a minor accident where he simply drove through a red light, momentarily forgetting what that meant. When Scott found out about the accident, he tried to get his father to stop driving and just use ride services and home delivery for his shopping, but his father had laughed this off as unnecessary. Scott had not mentioned this problem to Kate yet because he didn't want to give her more to worry about.

The truth, however, was that Scott was now just as driven to find his father as Kate was to find hers, and time was clearly not on their side.

Durango

Peter and John arrived in Durango early Friday evening. It was cool for late August, and the sky was clear and bright. The smoke and haze recent wildfires in California had sent eastward had departed a couple of days earlier.

Durango was a quintessential Western mountain town. It was set in the Animas River Valley at about 6,500 feet above sea level and was surrounded by the San Juan National Forest. The dramatic scenery made it a popular destination for mountain bikers, skiers, and hikers.

There was a steak house in town that John and his family often visited on their way to Telluride. It looked like a saloon from a Western movie, with a couple dozen tables added as an afterthought. The walls were covered with the heads of every type of wild animal in the state that sported antlers. The owner did not stop there, however. She had taken her former golden retrievers to a taxidermist when they died of old age. They stood watch from three shelves of honor prominently positioned behind the bar. Hanging from their necks were brass plates with their names etched on. John affectionately referred to it as the dead-dog tavern.

John remembered the debate he'd had with Kate when she was younger over whether this was an acceptable way to honor your former canine companions. The owner won her support, however, when a year later, she came to the table and shared with his family just how much seeing her pups every day meant to her.

John and Peter walked into the restaurant and found a table near the window. John was glad to see nothing had changed, and the three golden retrievers were still on display. He was particularly glad to see that no new ones had been added. Peter, who had never been to Durango before, settled into his seat, having already been told the stuffed dog story before they arrived.

John had taken another dose of his medication an hour ago and was feeling better. They both sat back in their chairs and ordered a beer.

"Are you feeling better?" asked Peter. "If so, I'd like to ask you a question that has been weighing heavily on my mind."

John nodded.

"Well, before we order dinner here at this lovely saloon honoring lots of dead animals," Peter said matter-of-factly, "and since I'm assuming you're not packing a revolver and expecting me to watch you blow your brains out, would you mind telling me how you plan to kill yourself?"

John laughed. "You don't have to worry, my friend. My demise will be by the pill, and it will be fairly quick and, I'm hoping, quite painless."

Their beers arrived quickly and after they placed their orders, John smiled and said, "On a more pleasant note, why don't we start working on the more optimistic view of the future of mankind that you requested at lunch, now that your glass is more than half full and I am certain refills will be readily available and most likely not tainted with arsenic?"

Peter chuckled and said, "Why don't you kick it off, counselor."

"First, considering the fact you were most likely one of the only college football players in America who was a card-carrying member of both the National Organization for Women and Students for a Democratic Society, I am assuming that most of the rather unflattering statements I will be sharing with you tonight concerning our current administration will not offend you."

John held up a finger. "On a serious note, however, my attempt at prescience concerning the potential future salvation of our dying planet is not only something I think could happen someday but is also the path, I believe, we are already on. And, since I don't plan for my steak to go cold when it arrives, I also expect once again that you will help to make this into a conversation, not a lecture.

"As you and I have both learned from our professions, for any problem to be solved—whether winning a court case or building a surveillance system—we must first clearly understand all facets of the problem, including its cause, its accelerants, and its vulnerabilities.

"The problem we must address now is the fact that the human race is destroying our planet. The cause of this is twofold: It is man made global warming and equally man-made overpopulation. We understand the cause of both problems. We also understand that the global warming threat is being accelerated by politicians that deny its very existence. So, to simplify our discussion, and since we both understand the cause and the accelerants behind global warming and overpopulation, let's discuss what their vulnerabilities might become."

John paused and motioned for Peter to join the discussion.

"Well, in my view, John, global warming currently has no vulnerabilities. This is due to our reliance on the leadership of the nations of the world to slow it down or reverse its course," said Peter. "Having a president who denies its existence and who is in love with fossil fuels allows other nations that are so inclined to ignore it as well. The sad thing is that we had been making pretty slow progress fighting this beast well before the current administration put on the breaks completely."

"I wholeheartedly agree," said John. "So that means that in order to survive, we are going to have to make global warming the most important issue for everyone on the planet and develop a global consensus around this mission. We still have time to stop it—and perhaps someday find a way to actually reverse it. So that begs the question: What needs to be done to make this everyone's number one priority worldwide?"

"Well just replacing the current president and administration is not going to get the job done," said Peter. "The last president told us it was important, but obviously not as important as a dozen other problems he felt also needed to be addressed during his term in office. I honestly thought that pitching climate change as an economic opportunity to create wind farms and other sources of clean energy was a great strategy, but it ran into a buzz saw called the oil and gas industry lobby. These are the only guys in DC who are more powerful than the lobbyists we worked with in the defense industry."

"Well you wanted to have a more optimistic conversation about how the world can be saved, so I will give you my prediction about what could end up uniting the world in a real attempt to save the planet," John replied. "However, I don't think you are going to like the solution."

"If it means there is a chance for my grandchildren to live a full and healthy life and make it into their eighties or beyond, then I am all ears," said Peter. "I worry a lot about the world our children and grandchildren are inheriting. That is, when I am not worrying about the fact that I sometimes can't remember what I put in my grocery bag five minutes after I leave the store."

"Well if the future I'm about to describe is disturbing to you, maybe you will be lucky enough to forget everything I said by the time we get back to the car"

Peter laughed. "I don't think I am ever going to be able to forget any part of this twisted reunion trip of ours, even if I wanted to, so go ahead and put your crystal ball on the table and tell me about how the world is going to be saved."

"Before I begin, I want to tell you the reason I believe some of the most popular movies over the last two decades are dystopian dramas," said John. "I think most people know, deep down, that life as we know it is not going to continue, so while these movies are fantasies, many of them are also quite believable.

"Let me share with you now the plot for my own dystopian movie, and how in the end, the world could indeed be saved. Since I don't have time left to write the screenplay for this and you were the English major, feel free to take the story I am about to tell you and run with it when you get home. Also feel free to donate as much of the royalties as you want to our alma mater," John said, smiling.

Peter chuckled.

"My story begins with the actions of the Christo fascist oligarchy that is currently running our country. These are the billionaires and divisive pundits who are handing the president his daily tear-down-democracy to-do list. Their real goal is not to destroy democracy—that happened a long time ago. Their goal is to focus everyone's attention on the new tariffs, invasions, or some other crazy edict from the White House. This activity is meant to distract us and provide cover for what is really happening behind the curtain.

"Didn't you wonder how the stock market could hit an all-time high while a malignant narcissist with clear signs of dementia was running our country into the ground? You can thank one of your favorite horsemen, Artificial Intelligence, for that. AI is the new industrial revolution on steroids, moving at the speed of sound and propping up the stock market. Many of the nine hundred or so new billionaires in our country became billionaires either as part of this new tech or just by investing in it.

"AI is a game changer because it is going to solve the problem that has been a thorn in the side of every king, dictator, or oligarchy throughout history. Of course, I am referring to all those millions of annoying serfs and peasants . . . you know, poor people."

John paused as the waitress brought over their orders. John's food was still quite hot, so he had some more time to lay out his case before digging in.

"Just think how many of those primarily Brown and Black people we can make obsolete by using AI to automate almost everything we barely pay poor people to do. Robotics-driven farms, ranches, retail stores, food production, and delivery, just to name a few. Not to mention schools with learning modules and playgrounds but no teachers. Professional athletes with genetic promise being developed before they even enter high school.

"Corporate executives love this idea. Just think, no more unions, no more maternity leave, no more vacations, no more healthcare costs for the vast majority of what used to be their workforce, because the vast majority of their workforce is no longer there.

"Remember how I said that overpopulation was the second problem killing our planet? So if we no longer need so many people, how do you get rid of the poor ones who do not look like us or speak our language? AI could figure out a way to do that as well. All they need is another Ebola- or AIDS-style pandemic that would be particularly attracted to people with a certain genetic makeup or skin color or those living in a certain geography. A lot of people think that could never happen. But when both sides of the equator for hundreds of miles start to become a desert, and when ocean levels start rising, tearing at coastal cities, the oligarchy will have to have a plan for survival—and trust me, it won't be manning machine guns on our southern borders to keep people out."

"Do you remember the cartoon show we used to watch when we were kids called *The Jetsons?* Remember George Jetson slaving away, working three hours a day, three days a week at Spacely Space Sprockets? That, my friend, is where the tech oligarchy and AI are taking us. The good news is that your grandchildren and mine will be just fine in this new world because they are white and come from families with money. Black and Brown people will still be around, just not as many of them, and very few without money or academic or athletic skills.

"Oh, and if you think that America could never pull this off, don't worry, we will have lots of help. Most of the largest countries in the world are also oligarchies. The leaders of these countries also control the media and messages their people see every day, and trust me, they are all primarily 'cashists,' not fascists. Wealth matters to those in power and their enablers much more than the politics. Wealth buys power.

"So," he continued, taking another bite. "Once the population problem correction is well underway, AI technology can focus on powering its energy and water-sucking data centers with nuclear and solar power and begin to figure out how to remove much of that nasty excess carbon from the atmosphere.

"The market today loves AI. After all, it is potentially enabling the rich white man's dream of the perfect utopian future.

"There, my friend, is your happy ending to my story. A new world for our grandchildren to inherit with probably less than half as many people in the world, but clean air and no homeless folks sleeping on their sidewalks."

Peter was speechless for a moment. Then he said, "I'll admit, my head is spinning. I'm now trying to remember more about the dystopian books I've read and the movies I've seen, but it's hard to recall." He took a few bites of his meal, lost in his memories, and John let him be as he pondered.

After a few moments, Peter looked up from his plate and said, "John, I know your intentions were to raise my spirits, but I am afraid the potential genocide of hundreds of millions of people who do not look like us only makes me think that Adolf Hitler will be smiling in his grave."

At his statement, John nodded gravely.

"So," continued Peter, "I have a better idea for how to finish our dinnertime discussion and end it on a more upbeat note. Since I am sure, as my search online indicated last night after you called me, that you are quite active on social media, why don't I turn my phone back on for a little while and you can help me find some of the photos I saw of you and your family? I would like to see the pictures of your kids and grandchildren again. When you are done, even though I personally have been boycotting every social media platform for years, I can do a quid pro quo and open my phone's rather robust and family-centric photo library and share it with you."

John smiled, got up, and sat down in the empty chair next to Peter. For the next two hours, they leaned next to each other, laughing and sharing pictures and stories of not just their families but of places they had visited and things they had done since the turn of the century. It was dark when they left, and the tone of the conversation as they drove to the hotel in Telluride where they would be spending the night was upbeat until John's head suddenly exploded with pain. After he'd swallowed another pill, they sat quietly while John leaned toward the window with his eyes closed. The severity of his pain was getting worse.

As they drove, they could see the silhouettes of peaks and valleys made visible by a full moon. Finally, they arrived at their first night's destination, Mountain Village in Telluride, Colorado.

Telluride

Early Saturday morning, Peter woke up to find John asleep in the bed next to his. He'd had a difficult night, and at one point well after midnight, Peter had woken up to find John sitting out on the deck, facing the mountains and looking out over the village below. He had wrapped his head in a towel, trying to find some additional relief to his suffering.

Peter quietly got dressed and went out to the porch. When he'd turned his phone back on last night, he had discovered several missed calls and text messages. He considered turning it on again to check them but decided against it. It was best to leave them unread. He didn't want anything to weaken his resolve to see this mission through to its conclusion.

Peter had never been to Telluride. Their annual family ski trips had always been to Steamboat Springs. John had always talked about how great Telluride was and how much his family enjoyed stopping there on the way to or from Steamboat, but work and other commitments had always gotten in the way of Peter extending their annual family ski week.

John had said he wanted to take the gondola into town in the morning to grab some breakfast and then hike up the Wasatch Trail along Bear Creek one last time. He'd told Peter it was one of the most beautiful places he had ever been.

The town of Telluride was in a valley surrounded by mountains and flanked on one side by a clear mountain creek. The town itself was almost as beautiful as the nature surrounding it. Mountain Village, where they were staying, was a separate small ski town higher up and on the other end of the free gondola that ran between the two parts of Telluride both day and night.

As he sat there watching the sun just starting to rise over the mountains, he tried as hard as he could to remember the things they had discussed the day before. He was now well past the simple forgetting of names and places. He looked at his notepad and saw he had not written any reminders since he had left Maryland. He chuckled to himself and thought he probably should have written himself a note to remind himself to take more notes, but then he probably would have forgotten he wrote that reminder.

The thing that made Peter's growing signs of dementia most difficult for him was the knowledge that it would soon rob him of his independence. Despite the dark nature of this trip, he realized he was grateful to John for pulling him out of his current life, even if just for a weekend, and letting him feel once again like he was doing something important.

One of the things he did not remember until he saw it again was just how much he loved the sky in Colorado, both day and night. It was so clear compared to the DC area, and the air felt fresh and cool. He decided to give his memory a break for a while and just sit back in his chair and enjoy something truly beautiful.

An hour or so later, Peter awoke to a hand on his shoulder. John stood behind him with a smile on his face and said that he was sorry to disturb him, but he was hungry, feeling much better, and wanted to get onto the trail as soon as possible.

As they walked to the gondola, carrying the two sets of hiking poles John had brought with him, Peter felt happy that John was not only feeling better but was now willing to move their conversation from the coming apocalypse to a more upbeat set of topics.

John told Peter all about Telluride as they walked down the main street to the restaurant. This included stories of things he and his family had done there over the years. He was purposely avoiding his favorite breakfast stop because he knew that the owner would recognize him.

Later, as they started up the trail near the end of the main street, Peter began to feel almost euphoric. The more they talked and laughed together, the more Peter felt as though his lonely and empty heart was getting a refill he had never anticipated. Talking with John was not like talking with Scott, his only other close friend, really. He loved spending time with Scott, but there was always the relationship of father and son, which kept him from getting as close as he had always been with John. After just twenty-four hours, Peter was beginning to feel whole again and grateful for every minute that he was sharing with his once again best friend.

The Wasatch Trail was a long but casual hike. The trail ended at a small waterfall that was fed by snowmelt. *John was right*, thought Peter. The scenery was amazing. During the first mile, the path gradually rose until, by the time they got to the midway point, the creek that had been streaming just below them at the bridge at the beginning of the trail was now over a hundred yards beneath them.

———

When they finally reached the top of the trail, they took their shoes off and sat next to the falls, cooling off their feet in the ice-cold water falling over the rocks next to them on its journey to the town and beyond. They saw two older women wading through the water just below them. They were splashing each other like kids. Peter looked over at them, tipped his hat, and smiled. Both women just laughed and waved to them.

After ten or fifteen minutes, they put their shoes and socks back on and began the trek down the mountain trail. The ladies remained and took over their post on the other side of the falls as they left. John told Peter that he was surprised there were so few hikers on the mountain on such a beautiful Saturday. He attributed it to the continuous and well-reported assault of Western and Canadian wildfire smoke that had plagued the Colorado mountains for several weeks that summer.

As they neared the midway point of their walk back down the trail, their conversation was interrupted by the sound of someone calling for help.

Both men immediately began to run down the trail, trying as best as they could to avoid the loose rocks that made the hike down much more dangerous than the climb up. Peter quickly trailed behind John due to the two artificial knees he now had to contend with. At the trail's midpoint, they saw a young girl waving her arms in the air and screaming for help. John called out to her, and she spun around and shouted with tears streaming down her face, "My mother fell off the mountain! I think she's hurt!"

John and Peter both slid on the gravelly surface of the trail when they reached the girl. Peter had to grab the branch of a tree to keep from falling.

John rushed to the spot on the southside ledge that he knew served as a popular place to take pictures. Peter took the girl by the shoulders and asked her what happened, but before she could reply, John called his name. Peter joined him at the edge of the cliff, which was protected only by two small pine trees about five feet apart. With the stunning view of the flower-filled valley and mountains on the other side of the creek below, these trees had probably served as a picture frame for thousands of family photos over the years.

As they both looked over the ledge, they saw a woman about eight feet beneath them, holding on to a dead pine tree that was wedged between two large rocks. Over one hundred yards beneath her ran Bear Creek, which was both rocky and shallow. If she were to let go, there was very little chance she would survive the fall.

John surveyed the scene and called down to the woman to see if she could move. He could see blood dripping from her forehead. She looked up at him with her arms wrapped around the base of the tree and her hands locked together. John could see that her legs and feet were dangling freely over the small patch of ground behind her. From there, it was straight down to the rocks and the river below. She said she'd hit her head on a rock and thought she might have hurt her ankle. She was beginning to look faint.

John looked her in the eyes and, in a firm and comforting voice, said, "Please, just try to breath slowly and hold that grip you have on the tree. Don't worry. My friend and I will get you out of there."

Both men quickly surveyed the landscape between them and the woman. There was no way to get to her from either side. There was, however, one other small tree right next to her. The angle of the slope between the ledge where they were standing and the tree that was currently saving her life was too steep to safely crawl down.

John looked at Peter and said, "I am going to have to go down and get her before she passes out. You are going to have to help pull us both back up."

Peter replied, in a strangely calm voice, "Okay, how do you plan to do that?"

John grabbed his two hiking poles and snapped the plastic caps off their bottoms, leaving only the ground spikes. "I'm going to slide down to the tree right next to her, slowly, using these poles like mountain climbing spikes. She is only about eight feet away. When I get to her, I am going to hug the tree, reach over, and swing her around to me. Then I am going to carefully take my belt and lock it under her arms so that I have a grip on her in case she loses consciousness. So do you think you can get us back up?"

Peter looked at John and nodded. "Okay, so if I tie my own belt around the base of that pine tree on our left and grab hold of it, I can swing myself over the ledge. You should be able to reach my ankles. After that, you are going to have to just grab any part of me you can and use me as a ladder. When you get to the point where you can grab the belt I am holding, I will let go with one hand and help you to shove her over the side of this ridge." He paused. "The only other option is to call 911 and wait for help, but she doesn't look too good right now, and if she passes out or loses her grip, she'll die."

"I agree," said John, and with that he grabbed the two poles, snapped off the plastic protectors, and drove them into the ground at the edge of the ledge as hard as he could. John then slid his legs over the side and grabbed hold of the two poles. Fortunately for John, he was six foot two, so when both poles snapped loose immediately, he was only a few feet from the other tree, and he managed to stop his slide with the not particularly comfortable option of spreading his legs and allowing his crotch to serve as his brakes.

After groaning momentarily, he got to his knees and, using the tree for leverage, brought himself upright while laying flat. He then reached over with one hand, grabbed the young woman's wrist, and told her to let go of the other tree and let him pull her to his side. She let go of her hold, and John pulled her up next to him with one hand, holding a tree branch with his other. He held her tight and explained that he was going to secure her to him with his belt, but she said she could just put her arms around his neck if that was okay. She did that immediately and promised she would not let go. Once she was positioned on his back with her hands around her neck, John looked up and saw Peter's ankles dangling well within reach. He took a deep breath, positioned his feet, and lunged sideways, reaching up and grabbing Peter's ankles as he fell back against the ground, quickly spinning to protect his passenger. Digging his boots into the ground, he slowly climbed over the top of Peter's legs, until he was lying on top of Peter's back. John's passenger could see her daughter only a couple of feet above her.

Just then, Peter and John were both surprised to see two arms and a different woman's head leaning over the ledge and grabbing at the women who was currently wrapped around John's neck.

She let go and was quickly pulled to safety by one of the elderly women they had seen at the top of the trail. The woman's friend was behind her, her boots wedged against a rock while she held on to her friends ankles.

Once their passenger was safe, both John and Peter pulled and clawed their way back over the ledge. They saw the woman's head wound was already being cleaned and treated by the elderly woman who had pulled her up. She looked over at them and said, "Don't worry, fellas, I'm a doctor. She is going to be fine, but I'm pretty sure she is going to need a couple of stitches. We called 911, and a rescue ATV is on its way to take her down to town."

The woman's daughter was sitting on the ground next to her mother with her arms wrapped around her, sobbing. The woman who had served as the doctor's anchor walked over to Peter and John with a smile on her face and held out her hand to introduce herself. "I'm Suzanne, and that lady over there is my partner, Rebecca," she said. "I am also a doctor, but I'm actually a psychiatrist, and I wanted you to know that, in my professional opinion, you are both certifiably insane."

All three of them laughed, and Peter told her that her diagnosis was spot on. He then opened his notepad, jotted down something on the page, and handed it to her.

"Suzanne, I really wish we had time to stick around and get to know you two warriors a little better, but we have a flight to catch out of Montrose. Since you guys have this under control, we're going to head back to our hotel. If you need to reach us for any reason, you have our names and my phone number on that piece of paper. I'm Peter, and this rather impetuous young fellow is John."

Before departing, they went over and introduced themselves to the doctor, her patient, and the daughter. They made light of the rescue, said their goodbyes, picked up the remaining set of poles, and headed back down the trail toward town.

As they moved out of sight, John said, "Why the hurry, Peter? I hadn't planned for us to leave for Glenwood Springs until after lunch."

"You must be kidding me," replied Peter. "You are the one who's been going out of his way to make sure no one knows where we are. Don't you think that our daring rescue is about to end up on the local news and leap from there straight to social media?"

John paused for a moment. "Sorry, you are right. But since we are traveling incognito, I don't understand why you gave that woman our names and your phone number."

"I didn't. I wrote down John Costello and Peter Abbott and gave her my landline phone number from thirty years ago."

"Abbott and Costello, huh," said John with a chuckle. "You may be losing you memory, but you sure as hell haven't lost your sense of humor."

Just before they got down to the trailhead, they had to move over to make room for the emergency ATV with two riders and a stretcher that raced by them, heading up the trail.

"Abbott and Costello, huh," repeated John, after they got onto the gondola. "That is pretty damn hilarious. The truth is, however, that we probably looked more like a couple of clowns than rescuers. I am truly grateful I will be gone soon and will not have to live with the memory of me thinking I could rappel down that slope with a pair of fifty-dollar hiking poles. The pain I am still feeling in my groin will have to be my punishment."

Peter laughed. "You have my sympathy, my friend."

"Also, since you are now the master of forgetting stuff, could you please just wipe this whole fiasco from your mind?"

"What fiasco?" Peter said with a grin on his face.

For the remainder of the gondola ride, they both just leaned back to watch as the beautiful town of Telluride got smaller and smaller as they rose up the mountain, until it disappeared completely as the gondola swung over the mountaintop. They moved to the seat on the other side so they could enjoy the equally amazing view as the gondola continued on its way back to Mountain Village.

Glenwood Springs

It was just before noon when Peter and John checked out of their hotel. Before departing, they walked through the village square and sat down outside a sandwich shop to grab a bite to eat. John's pain was coming back, and he left half of his sandwich on the plate as they left. It was about a three-and-a-half-hour drive to Glenwood Springs, and John told him there was no hurry as they got into the car. Peter turned on the jazz station on SiriusXM they had been listening to when they weren't in conversation.

They had both discovered jazz music from their friend Michael, who had roomed with them in a house off campus their sophomore year at Davidson. Like most of their friends, they had both grown up listening to pop music. But Michael's eclectic but amazing album collection introduced them to music that did so much more than make them tap their feet.

As a John Coltrane track came on, Peter's memory came alive, as it often did when he heard a piece of music he loved. He looked over to say something to John, but he was asleep, so Peter just turned down the volume so his friend could rest.

As their trip had progressed, he'd realized that being around John was bringing back memories of not just their time together in college but the times they had spent together as young men, building their families and their careers. Peter kept trying hard not to keep blaming himself for having let such a friendship disappear for so long.

The drive to Glenwood Springs was just as beautiful as most trips through the central and western parts of the state of Colorado. At almost no point was a mountain range not in view. Entering and leaving Glenwood Springs from either the east or the west side on Interstate 70 took you through a simply magical canyon, the Colorado River on the south side of the highway and an active railroad track hugging the other side of the river.

Although there were no ski slopes nearby and it was not as famous as other mountain towns like Aspen and Vail, Glenwood Springs still drew plenty of visitors year-round due to the natural hot springs the town was famous for. John had wanted to enjoy this treat one last time and share it with Peter. They had plans to have dinner at another one of John's favorite mountain restaurants, which was just across the pedestrian bridge that connected the town and the swimming and lounging pools that were fed by the hot springs.

Peter had to wake John up when they arrived at the parking lot of the hot springs, which had been easy to find, as they were right off the main exit from the highway to the town.

John apologized for dozing off but immediately perked up when he saw where they were. The main hot springs resort was a collection of several pools that were all fed by the same mineral-rich hot water coming from underground. There was the lap pool, where the salty water tasted like you were swimming in the ocean. There was also the giant family pool and several small pools that were much hotter, many of which had places where you could sit under a hot springs waterfall and let the heat and water soothe your body and relax your mind.

Peter, not knowing that swimming was on the agenda, had fortunately packed a pair of gym shorts that served as an acceptable alternative. After changing into their shorts and purchasing entry passes, John pulled Peter, like a kid, right to his favorite small pool, which had the hottest and biggest waterfall.

Watching John wade quickly to one of the seats under the falls, Peter saw a look of joy on his face. He stood in the water next to John for a minute before joining him under the waterfall. He thought about how great it would be if the soothing and powerful water now crashing down upon their heads could serve as not just a tonic but a cure. Although he was, at best, agnostic, Peter did something he had not done for years. He closed his eyes and prayed to any god that might hear him to please take away John's pain and maybe even spare his life.

After over an hour in the water, they went back inside and changed their clothes. Peter followed John over the pedestrian bridge back to town. On one side of the bridge was the Amtrack train station. On the other was the main street, which ran north from the bridge up to the cemetery, where one of the town's most famous former residents, Doc Holiday, was buried.

John led Peter to a restaurant called the Co. Ranch House and chose a table on the patio. This restaurant was famous for their fresh mountain trout and elk dishes. John directed Peter to the trout side of the menu, and he was not disappointed. He told Peter that their Rocky Mountain trout was always freshly caught and cooked perfectly to bring out its unique flavor. Oddly enough, the location of their back porch seating was under the shade of the main street overpass, which was a below-the-highway community hangout that hosted local performers and free movies on Saturday nights. They talked about hanging around to watch a showing of *Point Break* later but agreed that they had both probably seen it too many times, although not in a venue as unique as the main street underpass in Glenwood Springs.

Tonight's two-hour drive to Steamboat Springs was intended to be the final leg of their trip. They were staying at their favorite hotel in town that night, and even with the help of Glenwood's soothing hot springs, they were both tired and planned on an early bedtime and an equally early walk along the river trail in the morning. After that, they planned to have brunch at their favorite restaurant and then head up the mountain.

As they drove east through the canyon, Peter was thinking that tomorrow morning on their riverwalk would be the best time for him to do something he now felt he had to do.

He needed to try to talk John out of taking his own life.

He knew this would be a selfish act. He had reunited with his best friend after over two decades, and he did not want to lose him again. He wrestled with this conundrum as they drove through the darkness.

The happiness he had been given thanks to this trip with John made him question his judgment in this regard. How could he let his best friend die on a mountaintop less than twenty-four hours from now? He had another hour or so to wrestle with this problem before they arrived at the hotel in Steamboat. As he thought this through, he also tried to stay focused on the dark and winding road to make certain he got them safely to their next destination.

On the Road to Telluride

Scott put his sketch pad back in his backpack as he heard the warning announcement that the flight was beginning its decent into Albuquerque. Right after the plane touched down, he powered his phone back on and waited to get a network connection so he could check his messages. He saw he had a text message from Kate, saying she had decided to meet him at the airport.

After deplaning, Scott jogged to the security exit. The minute he stepped out, he saw Kate waiting for him. They recognized each other immediately. Kate walked briskly toward him and wrapped her arms around him in a strong embrace. She told him she was grateful for his help and then surprised him when she said, "I know where they went. I will tell you about it in the car. It's parked right outside."

They both hurried out into what was, for Scott, an unexpected blast of hot air. Kate walked to her SUV, which was illegally parked at the curb, and told Scott to throw his bag in the back seat and hop in. Before she started the engine, she pulled an emergency parking permit from her dashboard that read "Albuquerque District Attorney's Office" and tossed it in the back seat. "I keep that around for emergencies," she said matter-of-factly as they took off down the exit ramp.

As soon as they were moving, Scott asked, "So where did our fathers go and how did you figure it out?" It was now after 11 p.m. Mountain time. Despite the late hour and the long flight, Scott had felt a rush of adrenaline ever since the moment he'd seen Kate standing there at the airport.

"They went to Telluride," she said with conviction. "I found out exactly where the gas station is where your father must have paid for a fill-up and snacks, and it is on one of the two main highways north to Colorado. That's the way we always drove to meet you guys every year for our family ski trip. We almost always stopped on the way at Telluride to ski for a couple of days because my family loved both the mountain and the town. We also sometimes took long weekend trips there in the summer to go hiking. I am pretty certain that if my dad is planning a final trip somewhere, Telluride would be his first choice. I put in the fastest route, which should get us there by sunrise. According to the receipt, they took the scenic route. The way we are going is not very scenic, but it is much faster."

"There's probably not much to see at night anyway, so the fastest route is definitely the best route," said Scott. "And time is definitely not our friend."

As they turned onto the highway north to Aztec, Kate looked over at Scott for a moment and said in a much calmer voice. "Scott, once again, I can't thank you enough for your help. Since this is going to be at least a six-hour drive, I suggest you take this opportunity to get some sleep if you can. I know you must be exhausted. Besides, there is no way I'm going to be able to rest until I find my dad. I promise you I will not nod off at the wheel. I am used to occasional all-nighters in my profession, and as you can imagine, my adrenaline level right now is pretty high."

"While I appreciate the offer, Kate, I'm willing to bet you my adrenaline level could rival yours right now, and I have no intention of closing my eyes until we find them both alive. I have a six-pack of 5-hour ENERGY shots in my backpack, and I am happy to share them with you if you do start to get drowsy. I can also take the wheel if you get tired of driving."

"Thanks," Kate said.

Scott was surprised at the uneasiness that he felt suddenly being in a car alone with Kate. In spite of the fear that he had about the trips eventual outcome there was another emotion that was washing over him that he had not anticipated. This woman had been his first unrequited love. He had a crush on her since he was old enough to have a crush though he had never let those feeling be seen. To shake his discomfort he said, "I would like to suggest that we pass the time we have in front of us tonight by reintroducing ourselves. Nothing we do is going to get us to Telluride any faster, so we might as well keep our minds as occupied as possible by doing something other than worrying."

He was glad to see this had tugged a smile of obvious approval from Kate.

"So," he continued, "if my math is correct, you and I have twenty-five years to catch up on since we took off our skis for the last time in Steamboat. The last thing I remember about your family was when your mother passed away. My mom and dad flew to Albuquerque for the funeral. As I recall, that was August 2001, just a month before 9/11. So, how about it? Are you up for an all-night chat session or would you prefer to listen to my somewhat eclectic music playlist?"

"You forget Scott, I'm an attorney, so I can talk for hours," Kate replied. "And you are right about one thing: Anything that would help to take my mind off worrying about my dad would be much appreciated. I have no intention, however, of telling you my life story in lecture format, as that would definitely put you to sleep, so let's try to keep this as interactive as possible."

"You can count on me Kate. And forgive me if I throw in an occasional joke or two. It's not meant to diminish the seriousness of the moment; it is a personality flaw you should recognize and one I simply cannot control."

Kate chuckled. "I remember that character flaw of yours quite well, and I'm pretty sure you inherited it from your dad. Don't worry, I am fine with some levity, just as long as your jokes have gotten better than they used to be."

Scott laughed. "Well, I can't promise that."

"Well," Kate said, "as you are my guest on this road trip, I will begin our story time with where you and I left off. Our last trip to Steamboat Springs was February 2001, which was just a few weeks after my mom was diagnosed with cancer. I knew about the diagnosis, but my little sister Kelly did not. Mom and Dad and I decided not to tell you guys about it during the ski trip because we knew it would be a downer for everyone.

"Since you knew my mom pretty well, I'm sure you remember that she was born with an infectious smile. Even as she went through hell that year, and in her final months, that smile remained.

"The suffering she went through fighting that disease is hard to think about, even more than two decades later. That year ended up changing both me and my life in so many ways. Before that year, I was occasionally almost as comical as you were, as you may recall."

"You were actually pretty hilarious most of the time," said Scott. "Since you were always taller than me, you used to bombard me with short guy jokes. We would get off the lift together, and standing next to me, you would look to your right and your left and ask if anyone had seen me."

Kate laughed. "You will get no apologies from me because you gave as much as you got. If I remember correctly, every time we headed into the chutes, you would yell for me not to forget to duck under the double black diamond warning sign that was at least ten feet above the entrance to the run."

"Guilty as charged, counselor," Scott replied, chuckling.

After a short pause and a sigh, Kate continued her story. "I graduated from high school in 2001. I got accepted at Harvard more because of my basketball prowess than my grades, and what should have been one of the best years of my life turned into one of the worst. Watching the most beautiful and loving person I have ever known die in agony changed me. Her last words to me were an apology that she had put me through so much heartache by having to watch her die."

Tears began to form in Kate's eyes, and she went quiet for a moment.

"I'm sorry, Kate," said Scott in a soft voice.

"So I left for Harvard the month after she died and the Twin Towers came down a week after I arrived. Honestly, the next four years were pretty much a blur. I played college basketball all four years, although we were never very good, even in the non-scholarship world of the Ivy League. I buried myself in my books so that I could ride a good GPA and my undergraduate athletic commitment to the school into a ticket into Harvard Law, which, fortunately, worked out for me. After law school, I came back to

Albuquerque and got a job in the district attorney's office. After a few years, that was getting old, so I left to take a job in my dad's firm.

"I know I'm biased, but my dad is a great lawyer and a great teacher and coach for younger attorneys. He is never flashy, he is always well prepared, and he has a presence in the courtroom that really moves people. After one of his cases, I met a woman who'd served on one of his juries, and she told me that she knew just by his demeanor in the courtroom that he was an honest man who would never defend someone he thought was guilty. I happen to know this to be true."

Scott replied, "My dad once told me that he thought your father was the smartest man he'd ever known, and that included his own father, who was off the charts. He also told me that John did his very best to hide that fact due to his humility."

Kate smiled at this.

"Speaking of humility," Scott added, "were you aware that your dad was also a great football player? My dad told me that he led his college football team in tackles for three years in a row. I'm willing to bet he never told you that."

"You would win that bet," Kate said, chuckling. "All he ever told me about his football career at Davidson was that he got his ass kicked for four years, but it paid for college. Fortunately, he got an academic scholarship for law school because his parents were both teachers, and they really couldn't help him very much financially."

"It looks to me like the apple didn't fall far from the tree when it comes to brains and humility," Scott said. "My profession has made me adept at finding people online and at digging deep enough to find out who somebody really is before we consider investing a lot of money in them. From what I can tell from my brief research, you have become New Mexico's legal rock star. I did a quick review of that hazardous waste case you won last year, and knowing very well the behemoth of a company whose ass you kicked, I must say I am more than a little impressed. Plus, you neglected to mention when you said you 'played basketball' that you led your team in scoring every year. I could go on about your other high-profile cases, rumors of your candidacy for public office, and charitable activities but I don't want to make you blush."

Kate quickly interjected, "Mr. Grove, I would appreciate it if you would not make me question my decision to invite you to join me on this lovely drive through the desert. I might have reconsidered that invitation if I had known you were going to digitally stalk me."

Scott laughed. "Okay, so I had some time to kill at the airport, and my curiosity got the best of me. I must say I am impressed that you have moved on successfully from your earlier vocation of trying to kill young boys by making them attempt to follow you down suicidal ski runs."

"Now you are going to make me blush," Kate said, smiling. "I must admit that I was quite proud of the many near-death skiing experiences I provided you over the years. But to be clear, that was only for you. I swear I never attempted to kill anyone else."

"Wow," said Scott. "Now I'm going to blush. I had no idea I held such a special place in your heart. I tell you what: After we find and return these two lost boys to their respective homes, why don't we plan a Scott and Kate revenge ski trip and see who the most dangerous skier on the planet really is?"

"Why, Mr. Grove, are you asking me on a date?" Kate replied with a sly grin on her face.

"Oh come on, Kate, you're not going to tell me that you didn't know I had a crush on you ever since I was seven years old. It was only the fact that you towered over me and gave me truckloads of shit that enabled me to keep my childhood obsession with you so well hidden."

Kate laughed. "Well, if that was the case, I must say your courting skills at an early age were pretty pathetic. You definitely gave out as much shit as you received. Let me give you a hint for any female pursuits you may consider in the future. The way to a woman's heart is not by unlatching her right ski halfway up the lift so she has to make it halfway down the mountain on one ski to retrieve it."

"I told you that was an accident!" Scott said, laughing. "The lift was packed, and I had a leg cramp."

"More like a brain fart if you ask me," she replied.

"Wow, counselor," Scott replied, "you really know how to hold a grudge. So since you brought up the subject of dating, I didn't see anything in my digital search about there being a current or past Mr. Badass New Mexico Lawyer. Since we're getting personal now, let's keep this ball rolling. Are you willing to provide me any information related to your current or past love life?"

"Sure. What do you want to know?" asked Kate.

"Everything you are willing to tell me," Scott said. "And by the way, you don't need to try to make it funny. I really am interested in reconnecting with you. And no, I did not just ask you on a date. However, if you should decide after this trip is over that you find me charming and irresistible, I can check my calendar for next month."

Kate laughed and replied, "You have not changed one bit." She paused for a moment and then said in a more serious tone. "The truth is there was more than one thing that happened in 2001 that had a big impact on my life. I have never discussed the second one with anyone, and I'm not quite sure I am ready to discuss it now."

"Okay," said Scott. "In that case, I have a deal for you. If I share my own deepest and darkest secrets, and you think I have earned it, I would be happy to listen to yours. If not, I will respect your privacy. But I will most likely die from curiosity."

He saw a smile appear on her face before he began.

"My biggest secret is one I have protected for a very long time now. My shield for this secret has always been my sense of humor. The secret is that I am really smart, and by that, I mean off the charts smart, just like my grandfather was.

"My parents found this out when I started reading before I entered kindergarten. They made a decision that I will be grateful for the rest my life. They decided to help me keep my genius status a secret as best they could and let me try to live a normal kid's life. I owe them big-time for not fucking me up forever by sending me off to college before I hit puberty."

Scott paused, gathering his thoughts. "Nobody wants to be that different. To be just like all the other kids, I developed a way to hide my so-called gift as best as I could. I purposely made errors on tests to keep me somewhere in the A-minus grade point average. I played sports, even played football like my dad in high school, but being three inches shorter, and thirty pounds lighter, my athletic career unceremoniously ended there. I stopped cheating myself on grade performance when I got to Davidson and when I left there, I headed to Wharton on a scholarship for grad school since my dad convinced me to pursue a career in finance as opposed to engineering. While math and analytics were my strong suit, he thought an MBA would be a better career path to follow.

"After graduating, I went to work for one of the big accounting firms and worked on a variety of projects—taking deep dives into corporations, looking for ways to cut costs and boost profits. I did well enough to get a couple of promotions and eventually got headhunted into a more lucrative opportunity working for a private equity firm in Boston. A few years later, I got an offer to earn my way into a partnership role in a much bigger firm in New York, so away I went. And that is where you found me, Kate, when you called. Just another New York finance guy working sixty plus hours a week, making more money than I will ever have time to spend and living in a small but ridiculously expensive apartment on the east side of Manhattan overlooking Central Park."

"You have my sympathy," was all Kate said.

"By the way, it should comfort you to know that my personality hasn't changed much. I crack jokes regularly and have become known around the company as the funny guy. What they do not know is that this is simply the best way for me to survive working for a cutthroat moneymaking factory.

"The truth is I'm not really that happy, and I'm not sure I have ever been very happy, at least since I left college. Davidson was a great fit for me. Not just because there were a lot of other really smart people there, but because the school had such a great 'everyone matters' vibe that you could spend those four years both being and becoming whoever you really wanted to be and still feel like you fit in."

Scott looked out the window, but there was nothing to see but dark desert. He waited for Kate to say something, but she didn't, giving him the space he needed to get the rest of his story out.

After a few moments, he continued. "As far as dating went, I was apparently attractive enough to get a date now and then, but I struggled to handle the next step very well. The women on our campus were definitely not there to find a husband, but understandably, they were interested in a relationship that had the potential to last more than a few weeks, which was my average girlfriend timeline," he said, sighing.

"Graduate school was so intense and went by so fast that before I knew it, I was interviewing for internships. The financial services industry makes it clear to their newcomers that they prefer you be a monogamist and that your true love be your devotion to them. My employers were always more than happy to have us work ludicrous hours in order to deliver the results they sought. Looking back on my lucrative first ten years in the financial services industry, I realize that if I had been paid by the hour, my overall compensation would not have really been that outrageously high." Scott shook his head. "When I finally moved far enough up the value chain to be provided some constraints on my labor, I had pretty much forgotten how to date, not that what little I knew in college would have been of any use to me in downtown Boston or New York. So I got used to living alone, and while I really do like women, the fact that I had decided never to get married and never have children was also a bit of a handicap."

At this, Kate looked over at him curiously before turning her attention back to the road.

"My father is the only person who knows the reason I have decided not to have kids. I am willing to share this secret with you as well, but I want to first warn you that this disclosure may cause you to decide to put me on the first flight home once we have completed our mission. The choice is completely yours, and don't worry, you won't hurt my feelings either way."

Kate looked straight ahead through the windshield and took a deep breath before replying.

"I am not afraid to hear anything you feel comfortable telling me, Scott. And by the way, your first secret was not very well hidden to me. I knew you were a different kind of smart as a kid. The dozens of conversations we had over those years gave you away. When we were not giving each other shit, we talked a lot about things teenagers generally do not discuss. I always looked forward to those conversations. In case you have not figured it out already, I'm not exactly lacking in my ability to read people."

Scott chuckled. "No, I suppose you're not."

"Even though you were two years younger than me, you always surprised me with the way you made me think about so many things that had nothing to do with getting down the mountain on skis. I never thought of you as anything less than a peer, despite the age difference."

There was a pause in the conversation. Scott sat there for a moment, looking out the window and into the darkness, and then let out a small sigh before continuing the conversation. "Okay," he said. "You've been warned. Your kind words make this a little easier to do.

"I also enjoyed our many conversations in the mountains. I always felt like I could discuss pretty much anything with you. I didn't have enough of an ego at that time to think of you as a peer. You were larger than life to me back then—and I'm not just talking about your height. I knew you were also really smart, and there were so many things I could talk to you about that I was just not comfortable discussing with my family or my friends. You always engaged and either concurred or argued, but you never made me feel like an odd duck for some of the thoughts I was having and the related concerns I expressed to you. Thinking back now on some of those reasonably serious conversations, I'm guessing what I am about to tell you will not surprise you that much."

"You mean like the conversation we had about Y2K and the computer crisis that never came to pass," said Kate.

Scott turned to look at her, astonished. "I can't believe you remember that conversation after all these years."

"I don't just remember it," Kate said, "I remember the concerns you expressed over the response by the industry. As I recall, you were pretty outraged by the rather tepid response of regulators. You were always passionate about your concerns about the future of technology and its impact on our world. While this was not exactly the typical conversation high school kids had during winter break, I found it fascinating."

"You could not have provided me a better introduction. I believe you of all people understand the curse of an overanalytical mind. It doesn't let you stop and toss things into the dumpster when you find yourself on a path that appears to be disturbing. Just the opposite happens. You find yourself relentlessly pursuing that train of thought. Once you arrive at a conclusion you are certain is or will someday become a fact, your mind can finally rest. There are no maybes. There will always be an outcome, and once you have convinced yourself of what that outcome will be, there is no going back—"

"I'm sorry to interrupt you," said Kate, "but I still do not understand what any of this has to do with your decision to live your life as a childless bachelor."

"Well, when I got to college, I focused as much on technology courses as I could as an MBA candidate. My dad told me the financial world was becoming an industry driven almost purely by numbers and analytics. Investment decisions that used to be made on esoteric considerations, such as brand value and leadership, were now being made based only on a more sophisticated set of numbers—and I don't mean stock performance," he clarified.

"The numbers that rule the financial world now are what analytics guys like me can come up with by digging deep into a company's cost structure to see how those costs can be reduced either by restructuring, through a merger, or by reducing labor costs.

"You see, Kate, paying people and providing them benefits is almost always one of the largest ongoing costs incurred by companies. This is where technology enters the picture. An investment in robotics that will reduce the labor costs involved in producing a car by 75 percent is irresistible to corporate executives, even if the company has to borrow a fortune up-front in order to build and implement that technology-based operational upgrade. No one even thinks about the impact on their employees, the ones who will lose their jobs when those new robotics are implemented," Scott said, shaking his head.

"I predicted the AI boom well over a decade ago. So did my dad. We both rode the AI stock market run up for a while, but then we both pulled our money out a year ago simply out of principle. Making money off companies that are helping destroy the world as we know it just didn't seem like a principled thing to do.

And this is where I answer your question. I believe, through my own analysis, that mankind is not just destroying the planet but is also on its way to destroying any semblance of a democratic society. I believe that AI technology will become a tool that eliminates tens of millions of jobs of all kinds. I also believe it will end up being used as a tool to eliminate human beings who the technology has made obsolete.

"I am choosing not to bring a child into this world because it will require them to decide someday, as a child born into wealth, if they will point their moral compass in a direction no one in my family has ever pointed theirs."

At this, Kate nodded thoughtfully.

While I intend to do my part to help keep this rather dark future from happening and to protect my family as best I can, I will not bring my own children into the world I believe is on the horizon.

So there you have it in a nutshell. I believe the future is bleak. As a result of this, I live alone, my best friend is my father, and I tell every woman I date up-front that I will never get married and never have children, which does narrow the field a bit. But you, Kate, are now the only woman I ever told why."

Scott reached down, reclined his seat, and folded his arms. After a long silence, he said, "That was exhausting. I think I need to take a break for a little while."

Kate looked over at him, and he knew she could see the anguish in his face. Saying out loud for the first time what he had carried like an anchor inside for most of his adult life had both exposed and exhausted him.

Kate reached over to the dashboard screen, navigated to her jazz playlist, and turned it on. The first album was Miles Davis's *Kind of Blue*. As the first song began to play, a smile began to creep onto Scott's face.

"You remembered," he said.

"Of course I did," said Kate softly. "Listen, I plan to stop in a couple of hours or so to top off the tank and take a short break in the last place that will be open this time of night. Why don't you leave your caffeine shots in your bag for now and try to get a little rest? You can take the wheel after we stop, and if you promise to try to get some sleep now, I will fulfill that quid pro quo by explaining why I also have decided to remain both single and childless."

"It's a deal," said Scott.

He reclined his seat farther back, closed his eyes, and tried as hard as he could to let the music from one of the greatest albums ever recorded become the tonic he needed to help him quiet his mind.

Steamboat Springs

It was just after dawn on Sunday morning when John woke up from what had been, for him, a relatively peaceful night's sleep. He looked over at the bed next to him and saw it was empty. Peter was sitting in one of the two chairs out on the balcony overlooking the river. John got up quietly and got dressed before opening the door and stepping outside to join his friend.

The two families had always stayed at this relatively rustic hotel in town. The view of the river and the forest was beautiful, and it was peaceful compared to the larger hotels surrounding the ski slopes. It was also a short walk to their favorite breakfast café, where they would all fuel up for a long day on the mountain.

As he sat down in the chair next to Peter, he could see a look of sadness and confusion on his friend's face. He also noticed his laptop was sitting on the table next to him.

"When I woke up to take a leak last night," said Peter, "I felt restless and confused, so I came out onto the balcony to try to clear my head. I looked at my watch and remembered that tomorrow was my daughter's birthday. I tried as hard as I could, but I couldn't remember her name. I don't know how long I sat here and struggled until it finally came to me. I felt myself getting angry and I've been trying hard to clear my head since then." Tears formed at the corners of his eyes. "I forgot my daughter's name, John. Do you know how fucked up that is?"

John replied, "I do know how fucked up that is, Peter. I also know you have been downplaying your cognitive problems since you arrived in Albuquerque."

Peter sat there silently for a moment and then finally turned his view from the river to John.

"It is actually pretty ironic when you think about it," said Peter. "You are dying from a form of brain cancer I can't remember the name of, and I am also dying—albeit more slowly and less painfully—from a type of dementia that has plagued my family for three generations."

Peter shook his head ruefully. "I probably should have told you the night you called me, but I didn't because I could tell you needed my help, and I didn't want to let you down again." The tears began to well up in his eyes again and his voice began to crack. "I've let you down for so many years, the same way I let down my wife and my family. I let my ego get in the way. America didn't need me nonstop for years to keep another 9/11 from happening. By the time I realized this, the damage was done. The people who needed me and whom I should have made a priority had moved on. I let you deal with the loss of your wife without the help of your best friend. I have regretted that for a long time and just never had the courage to tell you. I may have already told you all this yesterday or the day before, but if I did, I just don't remember."

With that Peter put his hands over his face, lowered his head, and began to cry.

John stood up, stepped behind his friend's chair, put his hands on his shoulders, and waited until Peter regained his composure.

He then said quietly, "Come on, Peter. It is time to take our morning walk along the river."

It was a beautiful but cool morning for late August. The trailhead was only a few yards down the walkway from the hotel on the north side of the river. It was still early, so they found themselves alone as they headed west, the sun slowly rising behind them. They walked along quietly for a while until John broke the silence.

"I would like to know about your diagnosis, Peter," said John. "I am once again your best friend whether you will remember that or not, and as such, I have a right to know. That is, of course, unless you can't remember what your diagnosis is."

Peter chuckled as he said, "You know, John, you are the only man on earth who could make me laugh about my own pending demise." Then he sighed heavily. "I was recently diagnosed with cerebral small vessel disease, which can lead to vascular cognitive impairment and vascular dementia. This was the form of dementia my father was diagnosed with. The doctor told me that there is no known cure and that it is indeed terminal. The only thing he could not tell me is how long it would take for me to become an angry and confused old man like my father was the last year of his life—or worse, an expressionless lump sitting in a chair for several years, being spoon-fed and staring blankly at a TV screen like my grandmother and my aunt.

"You might be surprised, but I was thinking about trying to talk you out of taking your life today on this walk. I have changed my mind, however. I have seen the pain you are in on this trip, and I understand now even better why you chose this path."

John looked over at his friend and nodded, understanding.

"The difference between where you and I are right now, John, is that the ones you love will not have to watch you die. I love and respect you enough to help you make sure that this happens. My fate is different. I know this from having been the one responsible for caring for my demented relatives. My children and grandchildren will not see me suffer; they will just see me gradually disappear. They will feel obligated to visit me occasionally, even though Iill no longer know who they are. This will continue until the time comes when I am no longer able to converse at all. There is also a good chance that no one but Scott will come see me once I become an angry old man that no one recognizes.

Peter looked out across the river. "This is what is ahead of me. It's a shame that we don't have the same heart or courage the Canadians had when it comes to letting terminal patients plan and schedule their own demise. Here in America, the self-righteous, so-called Christians who currently drive our country's agenda would never allow such a horrible thing to happen."

John replied, "I looked at that option in a couple of Western states that have a similar provision, but that would not work for me. Kate would fight me every step of the way, and I didn't have the time. Isn't it ironic that we can take the dogs and cats we love to a vet when they can no longer walk or live a meaningful life, but we can't do the same for the people we love?"

Peter stopped and turned to face John and said almost matter of factly, "I hope that this does not come as a too much of a shock to you, but I have decided to join you John. You told me that you had enough of those pills to kill a dozen people. My mind is still together enough to know that this is the right thing for me to do.

John stood there looking strangely calm and replied, "What is mine is yours Peter, and I am not going to try and talk you out of it now that I understand your diagnosis. I am not that big a hypocrite."

Peter looked into his friends eyes and just wrapped his arms around him and said with his voice cracking, "Thank you."

"I have an idea," said John. "Instead of wasting a perfectly beautiful day obsessing about how it is going to end, why don't we just talk about the things we have loved in this life. I'm not just talking about the people; I'm talking about the songs and the movies and the sights and the moments. I can help you if you have forgotten the name of a favorite song or artist. I will gladly be your surrogate memory. To keep it interesting, we can even have one of our always lively debates about what things we think deserve a top five rating on our scoreboard of life."

"That sounds wonderful, my friend. Peter replied

We have a lot of time this morning between the trail and brunch, so we should be able to cover a pretty wide variety of topics."

And so, they did.

As they walked together up the riverside and back to the restaurant, they remembered their lives both together and apart by sharing the things that had filled those lives with the most joy and meaning.

The debate over their top five movies and top five albums was particularly drawn out, but there was very little debate over the best moments the two of them had spent together. The problem they struggled with most was the fact that they could have made the best moments together a top fifty list.

When they returned to the hotel to check out, they were both in good spirits. They continued to discuss and debate memories of interest over brunch and on the drive to the parking lot located at the base of the mountain. They had picked up a new set of hiking poles in town after they finished their brunch to replace the ones that were now somewhere in the river in Telluride. Shouldering their backpacks, they started up the trail to the top of the mountain, side by side. As planned, they would have plenty of time to reach their final destination before dusk. It was a beautiful day, and they were in no hurry.

Telluride at Dawn

Scott woke up as they pulled into the gas station. He was groggy and surprised he had actually slept.

Kate looked over at him and said, "Good morning, sleeping beauty."

He looked at the dashboard screen and saw they were still a couple of hours away from Telluride. It was much darker now, as the clouds had apparently done away with the moonlight that had been providing at least some shadows of the terrain they had traveled through.

This twenty-four-hour store was part gas station, part souvenir shop, and part junk food emporium. Kate started to pump gas as Scott stumbled out of the car and headed straight to the restroom. When he stepped back out into the store, he did not see Kate, so he began to wander through the aisles, looking for something to eat that wouldn't put him back to sleep. He found an ample jerky selection in the second aisle, so he grabbed a couple of packs and headed to the nuts shelf. As he glanced to his left, he saw Kate walking toward him carrying a large bag of buffalo jerky. She looked at him and smiled. "A fellow protein junkie, I see."

"How else do you think I stay so incredibly fit and attractive?" he replied, a grin on his face.

Kate laughed and then pointed to a large jar of cashews and said, "I want those, and I am happy to share." After a brief argument over the best energy drink brand and who would pay for the food, they took a couple of laps around the building to stretch their legs before they got back on the road. Kate agreed to let Scott take the wheel for the remainder of the drive to Telluride.

"You should try to get some sleep yourself," Scott said.

"No chance," Kate replied before popping down a few more cashews. "We're only a couple of hours away. Besides, I need to consume the remainder of my protein fix along with this twenty-ounce energy drink. I noticed by reading the label that it guarantees to keep you awake, which I believe it will considering the unrecognizable chemical ingredients I am swallowing"

"Okay then. I gave you an out and you didn't take it. It looks like you're going to have to provide that quid pro quo you promised me and fill me in on the Katherine Eastman facts that can't be discovered on the web."

Kate faked a long, exasperated sigh, then said, "To begin, I want to tell you that my dad is also my best friend and always has been, so it seems you and I both share this not exactly common situation, particularly for a couple of over forty adults. That is the reason I need to find him. I admit that the fact that he is my father complicates our relationship from time to time, but there simply is no one in this world I am closer to."

Scott nodded, understanding completely.

"I will begin my story by telling you that I have been misunderstood by a lot of people for most of my life. I have never been an outgoing person, and yet I am clearly not an introvert. I believe I have a fairly well-developed ability to help people as an attorney, and yet I do not think I am egotistical. Self-confidence, particularly in a female professional, often gets mistaken for ego," she said, shaking her head.

"Here is what I will share with you: For as long as I can remember, I was good at things. I was good at sports. I was good at school. I also was told I was good-looking, which is supposed to matter to teenage girls and young women more than anything else, and yet I can honestly say it never mattered that much to me.

"I have always been keenly aware that we live in a patriarchy. Quite honestly, I have lived my life in a quiet defiance of that patriarchy. I love to win cases, however, I really love to win cases when my opponent is an arrogant male prosecutor who can't look me in the eyes because he is too busy checking out my body. By the way," she added, holding up a finger, "before you jump to conclusions, I am not a lesbian. I will get to the less important topic of sex in a moment.

"My mother gave birth to two daughters and then had to stop there for health reasons. She was such a beautiful woman, both inside and out, and she was also both proud and happy to be a woman. My sister is a lot like her. I, on the other hand, became my father's only son. I'm not sure if that was his choice or mine. Sports were a passion for me early on in my life, and my dad was always there cheering for me, at every race and at every game. The interesting thing is that I didn't ski or play basketball for him. I did it for me. I wanted to be the best I could be at everything I did. To say that I shortchanged my social life in the process is probably a bit of an understatement."

"I need to stop you there for a minute, Kate, because I am getting a bit confused," said Scott. "You and I were friends for one week every year for over a decade. You were outgoing, sarcastic, funny, and a lot of fun to be with—well, when you weren't trying to kill us both on the slopes. I'm finding it difficult to reconcile who you were all those years with the young woman you are describing."

Kate smiled and replied, "You may be surprised by this, Scott, but that mountain and our young friendship were actually really important to me growing up. It was the only time in my life that I ever felt free—and by that, I mean free from myself, and my own demands on myself. That annual week in Steamboat Springs was always one of my favorite times of the year."

Kate paused for a moment, and Scott chose not to interrupt. The road was dark, and they were beginning to head into the mountains on a two-lane road that was a bit scary even in the daytime, and even scarier at night. The pass they would travel through next was not well marked, and there were rarely any guardrails.

After a couple of minutes, Kate took a sip of her energy drink, grimaced at the taste, and then continued her story. "You asked me why I am single and, like you, plan not to have children, and I have been chatting about unrelated topics, so let me answer your question now. It began with the way I lost my virginity my senior year of high school. While, like most fairly popular kids, I went to parties occasionally, I did not drink and never really dated. Let's face it, I am six feet tall in flats and could probably have kicked most of my male classmates' asses if push came to shove." Kate chuckled, and Scott smiled over at her.

"In January my senior year that great American tradition called the senior prom rolled around, and I felt compelled to participate. I was asked to go by a six-foot-four tight end who was headed to Arizona on a football scholarship. He seemed like the logical choice, since we would look properly proportioned in our prom pictures.

"I had decided in advance that it was time to lose my virginity and see what this sex thing that was consuming my peers was all about. To say that it did not go well is a bit of an understatement." She took another sip of her energy drink. "It really was not my date's fault. He was clearly experienced and apparently used to his partners displaying nothing but pleasure and pride at being fucked by a good-looking football star. I, on the other hand, bled from the experience and quite frankly found it a bit off-putting having a massive man almost suffocate me while he rams his extremely large dick inside me with the tenderness of a sledgehammer," she said, shaking her head and frowning at the memory. "While this experience did not keep me from ever having sex again, it did keep me from ever wanting a man to have that kind of power over me ever again—"

"I don't mean to interrupt this tender and romantic story," said Scott, "but I do feel compelled to let you know, if you don't already, that there is a world of potentially available sexual partners out there on social media—and I am talking about normal people, not troglodytes. I can also guarantee you that if you prefer to assume a more dominant position when having sex, I am certain there are plenty of guys of all sizes who would be more than delighted to just lay on their backs and let you do the dirty work."

Kate broke up laughing at this. Wiping a small tear from her eye, she said, "I really appreciate the advice, and I will certainly give that some consideration should the urge strike me." Then she was quiet for a moment. "The truth is that, with most men, I find it difficult to forgive them for being men, and therefore there really isn't much of a chance for the relationship to go very far. It's so hard for a guy to convince me that he is not part of the patriarchy when it's so obvious that the primary objective of every relationship is to put me on my back eventually. This may seem to be a simplistic view, but it is based on more than just casual observation.

"Let me shift gears now and move to the topic of children. If children did not have to be born either male or female, I probably would have found a way to have a couple of them. Unfortunately, for the most part, those are the only two options. If I had a daughter, she would face a world full of men who don't want to share power with women, let alone relinquish it. She would always be judged first by her appearance, not her talent. If I had a son, he would be born into that patriarchy and I would have to fight to keep him from becoming one of them. If I won that battle, he would most likely eventually find himself ostracized and alone. If he chose to become just another misogynist asshole I would have to live with that somehow and I am not sure that I could."

At this, Scott nodded but kept his eyes on the road.

"I have mapped out my personal journey from female jock to career professional to spinster someday, and I am okay with it. I have filled my life with my love of my family, my dogs, and a few good friends, as well as the knowledge that every day I go to work, I will have a chance to win a court case that will make a difference. Sometimes that difference is just for one person. Maybe someday, that difference will affect all of us.

"You said you didn't live a happy life, Scott, and that makes me very sad. However, I must admit that it would be a stretch for me to suggest I live a happy life myself. I have instead reconciled myself to living one that is meaningful. I inherited that perspective on life from my dad, particularly after my mother died."

There was a very long silence as they drove through the darkness. The shadows of rocks and trees slid by them, looking menacing at night. Scott was trying to concentrate on the road, but it was difficult considering the conversation they had been having.

He thought about how ironic it was that people who were suffering often found comfort from friends or family who were also suffering. This was yet another flaw in human nature he would attempt to analyze and understand. Learning about Kate's own choice of a childless life not only made him feel better about his own choice but brought him even closer to her.

In Scott's mind, however, he had decided long ago that Kate had no flaws.

She was perfect, and he was surprised to find himself occasionally struggling with his words when in conversation with her. He didn't know what to do with this realization. Had he known this already and just buried it when she disappeared from his life, or was it a new realization?

He felt an uneasiness and a kind of confusion that was new to him. He also knew attempting to joke about it would be insulting to them both.

Scott glanced briefly at Kate and said quietly, "It appears we are kindred spirits, you and I. You have both my admiration and my respect for the courage to travel the path you have chosen. In some ways, you also have my sympathy."

"Thank you, Scott," Kate said softly.

"I do have to admit to you, however, that there is something good that has already come from your disclosures. If it turns out that my rather dark projections about the future are wrong, it will most likely be because of the work of strong and compassionate people like you."

In that moment, they both recognized they had not just been reunited on this drive but their relationship had, in a matter of hours, become much more important to them than it had ever been in the past.

For the remainder of the drive, they found themselves more relaxed and talked about everything and anything that came to their minds. Sometimes they laughed, sometimes they fumed at the cruelty that had become politically correct, but the conversation was never dull.

As they turned into the canyon leading into Telluride, the sun was beginning to rise, and they were rewarded with a kind of unique natural beauty that was difficult to describe but impossible to ever forget.

Steamboat Springs, the Mountain

Neither John nor Peter needed a map to find their way to the top of their favorite run.

It was nearly midday, and the weather was perfect for a hike. A cool mountain breeze met them on their way. John had weathered another headache while they were finishing their brunch in town but was feeling better.

Peter, on the other hand, as much as he had enjoyed their morning together, was feeling confused and was doing his best to hide it. While he had done well remembering many of the things they had discussed, he had found himself nodding and pretending to remember many others. He was pretty sure John had noticed, and he had frequently jumped in to help him cover it up.

Forgetting the names of certain songs and movies didn't bother him. It was forgetting so many of the places they had been and times they had spent together that made him the saddest. However, he found himself able to take great pleasure from John's own impeccable recall and the happiness he displayed as he talked about the moments they had shared.

It had been twenty-five years since John and Peter had been on this mountain together and even thought they had enjoyed its unmatched beauty together with their families for so many years this last visit would belong to just them—so they thought.

Telluride

As Kate and Scott drove through the canyon where Telluride was cradled, Scott looked over at Kate and asked, "So what's the game plan?"

"We're going to make an early-morning house call on a friend of mine who lives here," Kate replied. "She and her husband own the best breakfast and lunch restaurant in town. It was one of our family's favorite stops when we would visit. If our dads are here, there is a good chance they came to this restaurant. If we strike out there, we will head up to Mountain Village on the other side of the gondola and check out the places where we used to stay."

As they drove into town, Scott realized that the pictures he had seen online did not do the place justice. The town itself, although quite small, was the quintessential Western mountain town, with every store and restaurant they passed looking like the set from an old cowboy movie gone upscale.

Kate directed Scott to turn onto a residential street two blocks behind the main street and pointed to a beautiful white wooden house at the base of one of the three sides of mountains that embraced the town. This is where the restaurant owner lived. They parked out front, and even though it was just past six in the morning, Kate walked briskly to the door with Scott hurrying behind her. Upon ringing the doorbell, they heard dogs barking but got no other reply.

"They're probably already at the restaurant," said Kate. "It's just down at the bottom of the street. They don't open until seven, but we can try knocking at the back door."

Once again, Scott found himself half jogging to keep up with Kate's pace as they walked through the gate behind the restaurant and up to the employee's entrance in the back. Kate gave the door one perfunctory knock and then pulled it open and stepped inside, calling into the kitchen, "Jen are you in there? It's Kate Eastman."

A woman Scott assumed to be Jen turned from the food storage shelves and stepped toward the door. "Kate, what are you doing here? You usually give me a heads-up before you come to town. Did you come up with your dad and his friend?"

Kate's face lit up at the mention of her father and she quickly replied, "Have you seen my dad, Jen? Is he in town?"

Jen stepped out the back door and looked over at Scott. "First things first, Kate, are you going to introduce me to your friend?" she asked.

Kate regained her composure, smiled at Jen, and introduced Scott as an old friend. Then she dove immediately back into her previous inquiry.

"You mentioned my dad and his friend. That friend is Peter Grove, Scott's father. We came into town this morning looking for them. Would I be correct in guessing they visited your restaurant for a couple of your amazing breakfast sandwiches?" asked Kate with a smile.

"Actually, they didn't," said Jen. "Please let your dad know when you see him that I'm really pissed off they didn't come by for a meal and a hug."

"I don't understand," said Kate. "How did you know my dad was in town with his friend if they didn't come by the restaurant?"

"I saw a picture of them both on the local news last night," Jen said.

"Oh my God! Are they all right? What happened? Where are they?" she asked, her composure now completely gone.

"Whoa," said Jen, the smile leaving her face. "You want to tell me what's going on, Kate? How come you didn't know your dad and his buddy were on the trail yesterday morning? And oh, by the way, they apparently might have saved a woman's life. She fell at the mid-trail overlook."

Scott looked at Kate in disbelief.

"Look," Jen said, "why don't you two come inside and let me get you some coffee? I will fill you in on what you apparently don't know if you promise to fill me in on why you did not know what I am going to tell you."

Kate looked at Jen with an expression on her face that only a good friend could read. She put her arm around Kate, walked her and Scott to the first table at the back of the restaurant, and brought over three cups and a pot of coffee.

"Here is what I know," said Jen, after she'd poured them all coffee. "When I got home around dinnertime last night, I turned on the local news from Montrose, and the lead local story was about two older men and two older women who had rescued a young woman who had been frightened by a snake and fallen over that photo stop midway up the Wasatch Trail. Apparently, she was clinging to a tree eight feet down and injured. Her daughter had screamed for help, and two older men came running down the mountain. One apparently slid down to the tree to get her, and the other one pulled them both up. Two older lady hikers also came to the edge and helped pull the young woman back to safety. By the time the emergency response team got to the site, the two men were already on their way back down the trail into town," she said, taking a sip from her mug. "Actually, I have a recording of the story, and I was going to send it to you since your dad apparently didn't want to be identified for his heroics. Here, take a look at this," she said as she clicked on a link on her phone and turned it toward Kate and Scott.

In the video, a young female reporter was speaking with the Wasatch Trail in the background. "The big story today in Telluride is the rescue of a tourist who fell from the edge of the Wasatch Trail. Thirty-nine-year-old Bethany Johnson and her daughter Kim had stopped to take pictures at the midway point when Bethany saw a snake, lost her balance, and fell backward over the edge of the trail. She was able to grab hold of a tree before a potentially fatal fall onto the rocks and river below. Her daughter called for help, and two men came running down the trail. One of the men climbed down to Ms. Johnson while the other man helped to pull the two of them back to the ledge. Fortunately, two other hikers also arrived and were able to assist in pulling Ms. Johnson to safety. One of the women who came to the rescue was Joanne Sullivan, a doctor from the Denver area. When we spoke to Dr. Sullivan about the rescue, she provided us with this photo her partner had taken of the two men talking with her after the rescue. She told us they said they were in a hurry to catch a flight and so they were not going to be able to wait for the emergency crew to arrive. The two men gave their names as John Abbott and Peter Costello. We have attempted to reach these gentlemen but have so far been unsuccessful. If any of our viewers know either of these two men, we ask that you contact our station. The rescued woman and her daughter would like to have the opportunity to thank them for their courage and for their help. This is Judy Peters, your reporter on the spot here in Telluride."

As the video ended, Jen said, "When I saw the picture, I recognized your dad immediately. I broke up laughing when I heard the names they provided. Come on . . . Abbott and Costello. Apparently, they were not waiting around for applause."

Kate's face fell and she began to sob. Scott jumped up and put his arms around her as Jen looked on in shock and said, "What is going on? I don't understand."

Scott could see Kate was trying hard to control her emotions. "My dad has cancer, and we think he has come here to die," she said in a broken voice. "We are trying to locate him so we can get him back to New Mexico for treatment.. I need to find him before it is too late."

Jen looked at her with an expression of both shock and sadness and said, "I am so sorry, Kate. I had no idea he was sick. I can put an all-points bulletin out with this picture of him to see if anyone knows where he is. I suggest you run up to Mountain Village and check the hotels you guys stayed at when you were here. Is there anything else I can do to help you?"

Kate stood up and Scott stood up as well and went quickly out the door. Kate gave Jen a hug and thanked her for everything. By the time the two women got to the back door, Scott was sprinting and already halfway up the street to their car.

He swung around to pick up Kate at the back of the restaurant. As they drove off, he leaned out the window and yelled, "Thank you!" to Jen.

Kate gave him directions to the Franz Klammer lodge, explaining it had always been John's favorite hotel on the mountain because it was in the heart of the town square and a short walk to the gondola and other ski lifts.

He fought the urge to blast down the main street but punched it after he got to the traffic circle leading up to Mountain Village. They arrived at the hotel entrance in less than ten minutes.

Kate jumped out of the car and headed into the front desk to see if their fathers were registered there. Scott started to follow her but stopped, realizing he had not checked his father's credit card charges since he had taken the wheel last night at the rest stop.

Kate was standing at the counter waiting for someone to answer the bell when Scott came rushing in and took her by the arm.

"We have got to go right now," he said. "They're in Steamboat Springs."

Kate didn't say a word and ran out the door with him to the car. He drove while she pulled up directions, looking for the fastest way to get there.

As they headed out onto the state highway north, Scott asked if there was anyone they could call in Steamboat who could help them locate John and Peter.

Kate just shook her head and said, "No. It's a three-hundred-mile drive, and even if we push it, that's going to take at least six hours. Still, getting there in this car is our best hope." Then she turned to Scott. "How did you know they were in Steamboat?"

"I pulled up dad's credit card charges and found one that had just hit the account," Scott replied, "They checked out of the hotel by the river in Steamboat early this morning—the same hotel we all always stayed at." He shook his head and said, "I'm sorry, Kate, I've let you down. I suspected that Steamboat was where they were going all along but you were so convinced that their ultimate destination was Telluride, I was afraid to argue the point. You see, Telluride may have been your family's mountain, but Steamboat Springs belonged to both of our families. Your dad asked his oldest friend to help him end his life, and I should have known it would be in a place they both had known and loved." He swallowed hard. "My guess is that they'll take the trail up the mountain to the entrance near the Chutes. My dad had a picture on his desk of the two of them wearing cowboy hats and leaning on the bench overlooking the range to the west. That picture has been on his desk his entire life. Your mom took that picture of the two of them that year that we did a the five-day summer family getaway that included river rafting and mountain biking. I was twelve years old that summer, but I remember almost everything about it."

Kate looked at Scott's face as he stared intently at the road ahead of him. The tears were beginning to well up in his eyes as he said, "I am sure your father is still alive right now, and I will do everything I can to get us to that mountain before it's too late."

Kate sat silently for a moment, then reached over and put her hand on the side of his face, brushing away a falling tear.

"I have made a career out of being confident and decisive, Scott. Most of the time, it works in my favor. This time it did not. This is not your fault. I wouldn't even have a chance to get to him in time if you had not flown to Albuquerque, jumped in a rental car, driven all night, and pulled up your dad's hotel transaction this morning. You have not let me down, Scott, you have given me the only chance I had to see my father again, and for that I will be eternally grateful."

Clearing his throat, Scott said, "We have a long drive ahead of us, and my adrenaline is blasting through my shoes. I need you to pull up Google maps and check for police reports because I am going to punch it. Pick a good spot in about three hours for a quick fill-up. With any luck, we will beat those two old guys to where they're heading, which once again I'm betting is the top of the mountain."

The Steamboat Trail

Kate and Scott drove into the parking lot outside the main chairlift at the Steamboat Ski Resort, and it didn't take them long to find John's rental car as it was the only car parked in the visitor's lot.

Parking next to it, they jumped out and looked through its windows, seeing two bags in the back seat of the car, one which Scott recognized as his dads. They both turned without saying a word and ran from the parking lot to the ski resort office located at the base of the gondola. When they arrived, the door was locked, and they saw a sign in the window stating the office was closed during the summer season.

The lifts were not running.

"If they went up the mountain to Morningside Park, they would have had to hike," said Scott. I say we get to the top as fast as we can on foot. I don't see any ATV's for rent here, and I have a gut feeling that we are running out of time." He grabbed a trail map from a container outside the office. "We have come down these slopes hundreds of times together, so we should be able to move pretty quickly."

They traveled as fast as they could, battling not just the altitude and the steep pitch of the trails but also the loose rocks and other obstacles that were usually safely buried in snow. They took turns leading up the path, warning each other when there were any hazards, such as gopher holes, that could result in an ankle injury. They moved faster the higher they went, as their adrenaline spiked and their fear of being too late propelled them forward.

Kate slipped on a loose rock near the midpoint, but Scott was right behind her and steadied her before she could fall. He took the lead without saying a word. Kate did not hesitate for a moment and was right on his heels. They cut through the woods between the trails to save time. With no path to follow, they made their way up and through trees, ducking under branches and having to tread even more carefully to avoid a fall.

They had both clearly thrown off the layers of change that their lives had made a part of them. They were once again those two young teenagers, only this time their destination was the top not the bottom of the mountain, and the stakes were so much higher than the fear of falling on the trip down had ever been.

As they got within a quarter of a mile of the top, Kate heard something and told Scott to stop for a moment and listen. They stood breathless, then they both heard what sounded like a song, faintly working its way toward them, riding on a breeze from the mountaintop.

The Mountaintop

It was chilly for late August, and the chairlifts were swaying gently in the breeze, surrounded by the tall aspen and spruce trees that accompanied them up the mountain. There were no other sounds but those orchestrated by the wind.

The sun was slowly working its way down toward the top of the peaks across the gorge, promising that darkness would accompany the silence soon.

That silence had been broken recently by a beautiful song being sung over and over again, but now that sound had been overtaken by a man and a woman sprinting toward the bench near the top of the lift, calling out the names of the two men who now sat on that bench together. The men did not move but just sat there in the middle of the bench, arms around each other, facing the sunset soon to come.

Kate and Scott arrived on both sides of the bench at the same time and saw immediately that they were too late. Scott rushed to test for a pulse on both men but Kate just stood there frozen, already knowing that there would not be one. She dropped to her knees, wrapped her arms around her father placed her head in his lap and let go every tear that she had left inside of her.

Scott just stood there looking at her and at his father. His tears were spent and his analytic mind was now briefly put to rest.

This moment was indeed as he had envisioned it when he jumped into the car back in Telluride.

A few moments later she realized something that her shock and tears had momentarily left in the background. Scott's father was also dead. She turned and looked up at him. He was standing there silently looking at her not his father. She stood up and immediately threw her arms around him and said in a broken voice, "I'm so sorry Scott. I had no idea that your father was planning on taking his life as well. I don't know what to say."

Scott replied is a strangely soft and gentle voice, "I knew, but I was simply hoping that I was wrong. I'm going to call EMS. Let's sit down over on that other bench and try and pull ourselves together while we wait for them to arrive. They sat down on the nearest bench and Scott immediately took Kate's hand in his before he spoke again.

"I need to let you know something Kate so that you'll understand why I am not crying my eyes out right now. My father was dying, just in a different way. He knew it and I knew it. My dad firmly believed that when you can no longer remember who you are or the ones that you love, it was time to go. The idea of spending weeks, months or perhaps even years, wasting resources keeping operational the body that had carried him through life once the heart, mind and soul that was Peter Grove was gone was to my dad simply ludicrous. He had no desire to remain alive when he no longer had anything left to offer to both the people and the animals that he loved and cared for.

Those two men chose their final path independently from each other and were lucky enough not only to not die alone, but to share that last moment with someone that they loved. I plan to defend that choice that they made every day for the rest of my life."

Kate said nothing. She wrapped her arms around him and that is where she stayed until they heard the sound of the EMS ATV coming over the hill toward them.

Steamboat

When they arrived back at the base of the mountain, Scott realized it was going to be a long night. A local news crew that tracked emergency calls was already waiting for them as they arrived, but they both refused to comment. After leaving the police station in town several hours later, they drove to the hotel where their fathers had stayed the night before and booked a two-bedroom suite overlooking the river.

They made arrangements for both men to be cremated locally. After throwing bags on the beds in their respective bedrooms, they began the long and arduous task of calling family members and letting them know what had happened.

———

It was nearly midnight when Kate, having finished her last call, got up from her bed, opened the bedroom door, and walked out into the living room. She had heard Scott making calls from the porch earlier, so she walked over and opened the door, but Scott was not there. She heard nothing but the sound of the water from the river below.

She walked into the living room and saw that the door to Scott's room was partially open. As she stepped into the room, she saw Scott was sleeping on the bed with his clothes still on.

She stood there looking at him for a moment, then picked up the blanket lying on the floor and placed it over Scott. Then she climbed into the bed next to him, put her arm around him, and within moments she was sound asleep.

———

Scott woke as the sun began to rise and the first rays of light began to peak in through the bedroom window. He felt Kate's arm around him and the rhythm of her body as she slept. He lay there quietly for a moment and then carefully slid out of the bed so he didn't disturb her. For a minute or two, he just stood there, watching her sleep.

He then walked over to the window and closed the blinds. He picked up his phone from the nightstand, pulled the door shut, and walked out to the porch, sitting down on one of the two large wooden chairs overlooking the river.

He had discovered the message his father had sent from the mountaintop when they got to the hotel. He had also seen that it had a video link. Scott had decided to wait until he got some sleep before he opened it. He had simply been too emotionally spent to handle listening to what he knew was going to be his father's last words to him.

He hesitated for a moment, then went back into the small kitchen area of the main room and brewed a pot of coffee. He stood there staring at the coffee maker until it was ready. He poured himself a cup, then walked back to the porch and sat down again. His mind was clearing, and it was beginning to analyze what had transpired since he had taken that first phone call from Kate in New York. He was trying hard to understand what it all meant.

He had only been sitting for a moment when he heard Kate's voice behind him.

"Thanks for the coffee," she said. "Mind if I join you?"

He turned to get up, but she was already settling into the seat next to him. He looked closely at her as she sipped her coffee and turned to look at him.

She had changed. Something was very different. He felt his heart racing. He almost stuttered as he asked her how she had slept.

Kate's eyes caught his in a way they never had before. She smiled and said, "I slept pretty well, thank you. It turns out you make a pretty good pillow."

Scott felt unsteady, beginning to understand what he was feeling, but he needed time to process it.

"You're the first person to ever notice that." he said. "I was waiting out here for you to get up because I got an email message from my father last night that must have been sent just before he died and while we were on our way up the mountain. There was a link to a cloud based video on a file that we share attached to the message. I found the video and downloaded it but in all honesty I was waiting for you to get up. I really just don't want to watch it alone. Would you mind watching it with me?" he said.

She nodded her head and the smile quickly drifted from her face as he got up and went back into the bedroom to retrieve his laptop.

When he came out of the bedroom, he saw Kate standing by the sofa, gesturing for him to join her. He opened it and sat back down, his fingers flying over the keys as he launched the video file he had downloaded onto his desktop.

They both stared intently at the image of Peter sitting on a porch in the dark with only the porchlight behind him in what looked like one of the same chairs they had both just vacated. They glanced quickly at each other and then back at the screen as the video began to play.

"Scott, I am sending you this video to let you know I decided it was time for me to go. I really don't think you will be too shocked to find out that I decided to commit suicide. I made this video for you so you could better understand why I am doing this now and what I would like you to consider doing for me once I am gone.

"I know that you already know how much I love you. You became my best friend when I deserted my last best friend, John. Ironically, I was just given an opportunity to rekindle that relationship before I died, and I can tell you that it has been one of the best things that I have ever done. For the first time since 9/11, I feel like myself again. John has given me something worth its weight in gold to me. He gave me a final mission that really matters, and he has brought back so many great memories that had already been lost to me before this weekend due to my dementia.

"I forgot your sister's name the other day. I sat there and struggled before finally giving up. I had to scan my phone directory to find her. Soon enough, I would have also forgotten her face, and eventually everything else that has ever mattered to me.

"My dementia is terminal, Scott, just like John's cancer is. Like John, I have chosen not to spend the final months or perhaps years of my life wasting other people's time and resources caring for a man who no longer exists. When I am of no value to anyone, it is time for me to go. This trip I have taken with John gave me an opportunity to not only be valuable one more time, but to say goodbye to this world with someone that I love.

He understood what his father was telling him, but still, tears were welling up in his eyes, and Kate was squeezing his hand. Peter was surprised to see that his father was reading from a piece of paper.

"I apologize for reading this to you but it has taken me several hours to finish this one long page. I get confused and find myself struggling to find the words that used to come so easily to me.

While you owe me nothing I am going to ask you for a couple of favors. You and I have both talked a lot about the troubled times that are coming for our world. Your keen mind along with my own understanding of the mistakes that my generation has made by vacating our responsibilities as caretaker for our planet, have left us both pretty hopeless about the future.

The first favor I would like to ask of you is that no matter how bad the odds are, I want you to put up a fight.

You are much smarter than I am, and I have taught you everything I know about the flaws and weaknesses of the wealthy and powerful. You have used these to become a very wealthy man yourself while remaining true to your values.

Find a way to fight this coming darkness. Try to find people with big hearts like yours to fight alongside you. I am leaving this world with hope because I believe the best in people can still triumph.

I decided to forgive myself for the "war against terror" that I fought and for the impact it had on the people I love. I know my heart was in the right place, and I never stopped loving you and them.

I have one final favor to ask of you. You already have my will, but there is one thing I would like to add to it. Once I have been cremated, I would like you to reach out to Kate Eastman and see if she would consider joining you on a trip back to the mountaintop where the local EMS crew will find us. John is also being cremated and I am pretty sure that he would support my request to have our ashes sent into the wind there.

Please make sure when you talk to Kate that she knows your father had no idea that I was considering ending my own life. I made that choice tonight and I already know that John will respect my decision. Please also make sure that she understands that her father loved her deeply and his motivation was clearly and simply to keep her and her sister, whose name I have forgotten, from suffering again watching him die.

With that, the image was gone and the computer sat silently.

Scott stood up after a moment, held out his hand, and said to Kate, "I need to take a walk on the river trail and clear my head. We have some time before the shuttle picks us up for the ride to Haydn airport. Would you care to join me?"

Kate took his hand, rose from the sofa, and said, "I will meet you out back by the gate in a couple of minutes. I need to get on my walking shoes on and finish packing."

Scott nodded, picked up his jacket and hat, and took the stairs down to the back exit of the hotel. He waited at the gate that opened to the path that ran along the town side of the river.

When Kate arrived, they headed north at a casual pace. They both remembered the trail quite well.

Scott said, "I'm willing to bet that John and Peter walked this trail yesterday morning before they headed up to the mountaintop. I remember that they always got up at dawn the first day of our vacations and walked along the river trail. It was probably their only chance to be alone and catch up on the things going on in their lives before all of us kids soaked up most of their time and attention."

Kate nodded in agreement. Then, with a casualness that caught Scott somewhat off guard, she began to talk about anything and everything, from those past ski trips to whatever caught her mind in the moment. Scott suddenly found himself doing the same thing, as though the trauma and the heartbreak of the night before were just another set of events in the continuum of their lives.

Eventually the conversation shifted to the challenge that Peter had left for Scott, to take on "the fight." They discussed in great detail what that meant and how they had both interpreted it. By the time they were through, they had completed the three-mile loop and found themselves back at their hotel.

The airport shuttle bus was waiting for them when they arrived.

New York City

It was coming up on two weeks since the night Scott had found his father dead. All the arrangements had now been made for a joint memorial service to be held in Steamboat Springs at the end of that month. Nearly all the members of both families were planning to attend. Scott and Kate had taken charge of the planning as they both had power of attorney for their fathers, and they had been on an evening call together almost every night since he had been back in New York. These calls had not been limited to funeral arrangements. Recently, they had drifted into more personal discussions on how they and their family members were each dealing with their loss.

It was Saturday morning, and Scott left the health club he belonged to at his usual time. The club was on the other side of the park. Scott had decided to join a few months after he moved to New York despite the location because it sat next to one of his favorite coffee shops. His routine every Saturday, regardless of his workload, was to lift weights for a while and then take a three-mile run through the park. This was followed by the purchase of a soymilk latte and a fifteen-minute walk home across the park, listening to music.

He took off his sunglasses as he walked up to the coffee shop counter to place his order. Before he could speak, he heard a voice behind him call out, "Could you order me another black coffee, please? You are a few minutes late today, and I already finished my first one."

Scott laughed, spun around, and nearly knocked over the two people behind him to get to Kate. She stood from her table in the corner of the shop to meet him. He held her so tight, he was sure he nearly took her breath away.

"Relax there, cowboy," she said with a smile. "You stink, and you better get back over there before the line gets any longer. And please make both of those drinks to go. It took me fourteen minutes to walk here from your apartment building, which should give us plenty of time to finish them before we get back. I'll wait for you outside."

Scott stood in line with his heart racing. A few agonizing minutes later, he stepped out of the shop and saw Kate standing across the street, apparently taking a picture of a church down the road that he had never noticed. She waved at him as he dodged several cars to get to her as quickly as he could.

"Wow," she said after he handed her drink to her. "I'm really impressed. The coffee is nice and hot, and you didn't get killed crossing the street."

"Okay," he said as they entered the park, "enough of the jokes. I'm supposed to be the funnyman, remember? Needless to say, and as you can probably tell from my rather embarrassing greeting, I'm really happy to see you. Why didn't you tell me you were coming?"

"To be honest with you it's because I didn't know I was coming until yesterday, when I found a flight that would get me here in time for coffee," she said, chuckling. Then she got serious again. "I missed you, Scott. The nightly calls were just not cutting it for me. I thought it might be a good idea to get together, now that we have had some time to recover from our last trip and talk about what comes next for us. That is, assuming you think there should be something next for us."

Scott stopped and just stood there for a moment, looking at her. Then he walked over, took her cup from her hand, and set both drinks down on the bench next to him. He then took both of Kate's hands in his and said. "I love you. If I sound a little bit shaky, it's because I am forty-five years old and I have never said this to a woman who was not my mother or my sister."

Kate smiled at him.

"To be honest," he continued. "I think I've always loved you, ever since I was a kid. When you called me that Saturday night two weeks ago, I felt something stir inside me that I could not put my finger on. Now I can. I love you, and I always have. So there you have it. I am not quite sure yet what to do about this, however, so I am open to any suggestions you might have."

His heart was racing as she started to walk with him, hand in hand, toward the east side of the park. The drinks were left forgotten.

After a few seconds that seemed like an eternity, she calmly replied, "I love you too, Scott, but I think you are smart enough to have figured that out when you saw me in the coffee shop."

He smiled at her, relieved. But she continued. "The pain I felt from the loss of my father began to subside a few days after he died. The letter he left for me helped a lot, and I have now accepted the fact that he had the right to do what he did and that he did it as an act of love. What surprised me was that a new kind of sadness was taking over, and I realized it was the fact that I was missing you dreadfully. The more we spoke, night after night, the clearer it became to me, and I knew I had to do something about it, so that's why I am here."

"And I'm so glad you are," he told her, squeezing her hand.

"Your doorman, by the way, is a charming man and was kind enough to stash my backpack until we return. I don't have to be back to the office until Monday afternoon, so I thought I would invite myself to spend the weekend with you. I realize I am quite a bit older and not as gorgeous as I used to be, but since we have both now admitted we are in love with each other, I thought we could try something out."

Scott stopped, grabbed her other hand again, smiled at her, and said, "Try something out. Just what did you have in mind?"

She stood there, looking straight into his eyes, and in a calm voice replied, "I believe they call it making love. As you and I have both observed already, it is easy to have sex with someone, but to actually make love, you have to have someone you love. And it appears we both now have the opportunity to try this out for the first time in our lives."

Scott once again wrapped her in his arms, this time much more gently, and tried as hard as he could to give her a kiss she would remember forever.

It was, and she would.

Steamboat Springs

Ten years later

Scott came out of the house with his backpack over his shoulder and a picture under his arm and waited on the porch for Kate. She came out a minute later with a bag also slung over one shoulder. Without saying a word, they smiled at each other, stepped off the porch, and headed to the trail that led up to the top of the mountain.

The two of them had jointly purchased this cabin three years after their fathers had died. It was a large mountain cabin with more rooms than they needed but always enough to accommodate members of both the Eastman and the Grove extended families. It was open year-round to any family member wishing to get away to the mountains, no strings attached, no limits on the stay. Scott's nephew had spent six months living there after he graduated from college. He spent his time both bartending and teaching kids how to ski. His niece was there that same winter with two of her friends during an extended winter break.

The cabin was serving the purpose the buyers had intended— to bring the two families closer together again and to make sure the memories of their times together, whether fifty years ago or just last summer, were always remembered.

Kate and Scott always came during the holidays, when the most family members were there. Skiing in Colorado in late December had become a bit dicey due to climate change, but it was mostly a place for the three generations of the two families to share meals, hikes, and board games. Kate and Scott usually took a five- or six-day annual ski trip of their own, almost always to a place where they had never skied before. Last year, it had been in Austria. The year before, it was Canada.

To their family and friends, the relationship between them remained a bit of a mystery, as they both chose to never discuss it. For ten years now, whenever one of them attended a charity or political event, the other was always seated at their side. No one had ever seen a public display of a romantic relationship and yet they clearly were so much more than just good friends.

Scott had left his New York firm eight years earlier and had joined a boutique private equity firm in Austin, Texas. It had been started by a former oil man who had become a leader in funding projects that were turning America away from fossil fuels and toward carbon-limited renewable energy sources. Scott had become the financial wizard behind building the business models that had convinced many detractors to see that this transition could be achieved without forcing the industry's billionaires to have to sell their yachts.

Despite the importance he placed on the work, the flight from Austin to Albuquerque was just over an hour, and Scott made sure that every chance he got, his weekends were spent there with Kate and her current dog.

The hike to the mountaintop where their fathers' memorial bench was located was only about thirty minutes from the cabin. For both of them, this had become one of their most treasured days of the year. It was a quiet walk taken by two people who had come to appreciate the importance of this memory and being together without the need for constant conversation. The quiet was usually only broken by the sound of the wind in the trees that surrounded them.

Kate had taken several younger attorneys and left her father's firm two years after his death to build a new practice focused on immigrant rights and the rights of every person in the state to have access to clean water and clean air. Her team had not only won two landmark rulings but had built up a sizable legal war chest that had come from two local, eco-friendly billionaires.

While her name had been floated for political office, she loved the work she was doing, and she had no intention of letting up or changing the path she was on. Devastating wildfires in the West and Southwest were now also showing up in the Southeast. The direct link to climate change had become impossible to deny as it had now left millions of people homeless and hungry worldwide. Rising sea levels had nearly destroyed two small island nations. The collapse of the climate change denier administration following a series of natural disasters and an AI-driven financial crisis had helped bring hope back to those who were working hard to make Earth livable for everyone, not just the wealthy. International collaboration in attacking this global challenge had also begun to grow again.

Kate and Scott were grateful that, so far, Steamboat Springs and most of the mountain region north of Denver had been spared from the wildfires. Telluride had not been so fortunate, however, and was trying to rebuild from the damage caused by two separate wildfires. This rebuilding effort was a struggle due to the diminishing annual snowfall and the impact this had on their winter ski season revenue.

As Kate and Scott reached the clearing near the top of the chairlift, they both smiled and took each other's hand, walking over to their fathers' memorial bench. It was well cared for and had a small bronze plaque embedded in the top wooden plank that said, In Loving Memory of John and Peter.

They sat down next to each other and opened up their bags. Scott got up and set the painting he had been holding down facing them, balanced against the small easel he had pulled from his bag.

He had taken the painting from the mantel of the living room fireplace, where it waited patiently every year for its annual visit to the mountaintop. Just above the painting were two bent and damaged hiking poles, crossed like swords in a museum. Each of the poles had a brass nameplate beneath its handle. The first one said Abbott. The second one said Costello. The painting had begun as the sketch on his pad during that late-night flight to New Mexico ten years ago. He had finished the sketch on the flight home two days later and then had painted it to give to Kate as a Christmas present that year.

It was so much better than the photograph. He had made sure their faces and their eyes projected the love of where they were, and of each other.

Kate had placed it on the mantel of their mountain cabin and there it remained, a picture of two young men in cowboy hats with their arms around each other at the top of the mountain in Steamboat Springs, Colorado.

Scott sat back down, got out his portable speaker, and placed it on the bench beside him. Then he opened his phone to pull up the only playlist he had with just one song.

When he'd gotten back to New York after that fateful trip ten years ago, Scott had discovered a number of notes on Peter's phone, His father had apparently wanted to retain, and perhaps even pass along, a few of the lists of their favorite things he and John had chronicled and debated as they took their final river walk together that Sunday morning.

The list included, among other things, their top five favorite moments together, favorite movies, favorite albums, and favorite songs.

The song that had been playing on his father's phone when he and Kate found them was their number one song, and had an exclamation point next to it.

Kate pulled a well-wrapped bottle of Scotch and two glasses out of her bag, then poured them both drinks. They held them until the song began to play. Then they met each other's eyes—tear-filled in that moment—smiled, clinked their glasses, and quietly said, "To the four of us."

Then they sat back and looked straight ahead at the mountains in front of them, sipping their drinks and listening to what had now become Scott's and Kate's favorite song."

The unforgettable voice of Nat King Cole singing *Nature Boy* spoke a simple truth to them in his final refrain:

"The greatest thing you'll ever learn is just to love and to be loved in return."

They leaned against each other and sat quietly on the bench until sunset. Then they got up and headed back down the mountain. The trees seemed to be waving to them as they passed, and the wind was clearly whispering to them a quiet goodbye . . . until next time.

www.ingramcontent.com/pod-product-compliance
Lightning Source LLC
Chambersburg PA
CBHW021403150726

47989CB00005B/2385